Brenda Storm
Finding Amelia Earhart

A novel by
Michael E. Coones

Brenda Storm Finding Amelia Earheart is a work of fiction. All incidents and dialogue, and all characters with the exception of some well-known historical figures, are products of the author's imagination and are not to be construed as real. Where real-life historical figures appear, the situations, incidents, and dialogues concerning those persons are entirely fictional and are not intended to depict actual events or to change the entirely fictional nature of the work. In all other respects, any resemblance to actual persons, living or dead, events, or locales is entirely coincidental.

Copyright 2023 Michael E. Coones
All rights reserved
This book or parts thereof, may not be reproduced in any way, stored in any retrieval system or transmitted in any form by any means without prior written permission of the publisher
ISBN - 9798871203828

The Adventure Begins
The Sinai Peninsula

Present Day

Throughout history, God has made his presence known to those who believed and paid attention. The cradle of his hand has always lied within Egypt, the wilderness of Sinai, and the baron lands around the Dead Sea. It is the homelands of the Lord's only begotten Son, Jesus Christ. Believers in God have lived humble lives near Mount Sinai since Moses. As shepherds, these modern-day nomads have continued to live as their fathers and their fathers before them have done for countless generations. Each day, doing nothing but the monotonous, mundane chore of watching the family's sheep or goat herd as they grazed upon the scarce wild grasses of the desert. But on this day, a young Bedouin boy named Isaac would have his life changed forever.

He was the youngest son in a family of six and studied the scriptures daily within the goatskin tent of his father, Emir. Isaac's nomadic life had taken him from one end of the Sinai Peninsula to the other. As his eyes followed a plane soaring overhead, he yearned to become a pilot and transcend his meager existence. He dreamed of rising above the arid sands and discovering a better future. A life free from the smell of goats and sheep. But this was not that day.

While searching for a stray goat, he had climbed to the top of a rocky peak and looked down into a valley of sand below. The baron pocket below him held something more than he had expected. A magnificent silver twin-engine Lockheed Electra aircraft stood, gleaming under the sun's rays. Its flawless exterior seemed untouched by time, exuding an aura of perfection. Nestled on the golden sand, it appeared like an angelic touch had delicately positioned it, radiating a divine presence. Its landing gear rested upon the undisturbed sand beneath its fuselage with no physical signs of a landing. As Isaac made his way down the side of the rocky outcropping, he began looking for the plane owners. He couldn't fathom the idea that they would forsake a stunning aircraft like this amidst the barren expanse of the desolate Sinai wilderness. His sight of its sleek and majestic structure stood in stark contrast to the desolation that surrounded it. The silence was deafening, broken only by the occasional gust of wind that whispered through the emptiness. The air carried a faint scent of dust and decay, a testament to the passage of time. As he approached the abandoned aircraft, a sense of awe and curiosity washed over him, mingled with a tinge of sadness for the forgotten beauty before him. Without thinking, he made his way slowly to the door on the side of the plane, reached up to its handle, and found it locked. He took a step back and looked up to the side windows of the cockpit. Was someone still inside? Was someone hurt in there? These were some questions he asked himself.

His family had seen oil company executives and other workers as they searched for unknown sources of oil within the wastelands of the Sinai. Maybe, he thought, this plane was part of that process. But for whatever reason, it was here now, and the owners were nowhere to be found. After bringing his father back, Isaac watched as Emir climbed to the wing and wrote a serial number he saw printed on the side of the plane. Taking that number, he gave it to his eldest son and sent him by camel to find someone with a radio set so they could send a message to the government authorities for identification. By the following day, Isaac, his family, his tents, and his herds were over fifty miles away, leaving the mystery far behind.

• • • •

Upstate New York

Present Day

It was raining as Brenda Storm sat inside the shelter of her canvas tent. She was a beautiful woman of thirty-four with brown hair and hazel eyes. A Professor at Princeton University, she held a doctorate in anthropology and antiquities. She was now here on the side of the Hill Cumorah in Ontario County, New York, in search of the sword of Shiz. She believed the artifact came from an ancient civilization that once inhabited America.

Brenda's eyes felt tired as she realized what little sleep she had had since arriving at this site ten days ago. After placing her GPS onto a sizeable topographical map, she marked off her last search area. Closing her eyes, she leaned back and exhaled deeply, finding solace in the soothing sound of rain falling on the shelter. The memory of feeling safe when, as a child, she would sleep between her parents on a rainy night now comforted her. She rested momentarily, then instantly opened her eyes at an unknown sound nearby. She moved forward, pulled one of her 1911 Colt Mark IV guns from its holster on her hip and listened intently. Because Storm had served in the military in Afghanistan for three years, nothing now scared her. She had developed expertise in marksmanship and received extensive training in hand-to-hand combat. Traits she never expected to use in anthropology. But stranger things had happened in her life. After hearing nothing more, she replaced the gun and grabbed a long-handled shovel before hesitantly walking back into the rain. In the twilight, she stopped and looked around but saw nothing but the constant falling rain. Her mind focused as she traveled through the thick trees around her to the following dig site. She pulled out her metal detector within a clearing and switched it on. So far on this expedition, she had found one old can, two sets of keys, and a Micky Mouse pocket watch.

After excavating down two feet, her shovel struck something hard, and a loud clang rang through the night. She then pulled out a small flashlight and shined it into the hole. Falling to her knees, she began digging out the dark soil with her gloved hands, and within a minute, she pulled out the remains of a sword. It had a hilt made of solid gold; its steel blade cankered with rust. When she studied it more closely within her light, she found the mark of Shiz upon the hilt.

Startled, she heard the unmistakable sound of guns cocking behind her. Storm spun around and went for her weapon.

"I wouldn't do that if I were you!" A voice cried out from the darkness.

She turned around again with the sword in her hand and stood face-to-face with someone she knew all too well. "Foster... I'm shocked it took you so long to show up!" Storm called out through the pounding rain.

"Why should I do any of the work when I have you to do it for me?" Foster Asked.

Dr. Sigman Foster was one of Brenda's oldest competitors for antiquities worldwide. He was Yale University's leading anthropologist and always seemed to be two steps behind her. He was a heavy-set man of fifty-six with an unusual streak of gray running through the center of his dark brown hair, giving him the look of an overweight skunk. His full beard, peppered with gray, enhanced his animalistic look. He held a gun of his own and smiled.

"Now... slowly place both of your weapons on the ground and move away!" As she moved to do so, he said. "Slowly!" Still holding the sword, Storm pulled her guns from the holsters and dropped them onto the wet grass at her feet. "That's a good lass," He uttered in his strong Irish brogue.

As the rain continued to fall, Storm spoke. "Not of great worth, Foster... Just a family heirloom."

"We be seein' bout that!" Extending his free hand, Foster pronounced. "Now, hand it to me." She turned her head back to see the other three men standing behind her and assessed her situation. "Don't be gettin' any crazy ideas, Storm… It's not worth your wee life!"

"I still owe you one for that little trick you pulled on me in Nahal Dragot!" As the lightning crackled overhead, Storm lifted the sword and advanced.

Foster fell back two paces. "You can't still be holdin' that against me, are ya?" He lifted his gun. "Come on, Storm… you must admit, it was pretty funny!"

Brenda shook her head. "I couldn't get that smell off for a month!"

Foster cocked his pistol and pointed it at Storm's head. "Enough small talk… I'm gettin' soaked. Just hand it over!" he demanded; his voice tinged with annoyance. Without warning, one of the gunmen struck Storm from behind, using the butt of his rifle, causing her to lose consciousness and crumple to the wet ground. Foster Picked up the sword and looked down at her unmoving body. "Thanks, Lass, I owe you one!"

• • • •

Princeton University

Present Day

As professor at the University, Brenda Storm positioned herself before her anthropology 101 class the morning she had returned to work. She was a dedicated educator and had taught her class even though she was still suffering from the impact of a slight case of pneumonia from her long hours in the cold, chilling rain. With a handkerchief in her hand, she continued her lecture.

"Masada, a hilltop fortress, was where the Jews made their last resistance against the Roman Empire in 73 AD. It lies twenty-five miles from the city of Judea and, strangely enough, King Herod of Judea built it in 37 BC." Storm turned away and sneezed. Wiping her nose, she continued. "When the Jews Revolted against Roman control, they escaped to Masada and held the Roman legions at bay." Storm began to sneeze again, but the urge subsided as quickly as it had come. "Their leader was a man named Eleazar and when he saw they were soon going to be captured by the Romans, he said this…" Storm hit a button on her laptop and the quote instantly appeared on the large wall screen as she read it. "My loyal followers, long ago we resolved to serve neither the Romans nor anyone else except our God. Now, it's time to prove our determination by doing deeds. Daybreak will see an end to our resistance, so let us choose death rather than a lifetime of slavery. We will preserve our freedom even unto death!" In the back of the room, a hand popped up. Noticing it, Brenda called out.

"Yes, Nathan?"

"So… what became of them?" He questioned.

"They killed each other and the last man alive fell upon his own sword."

In disgust, Nathan added, "That's kinda gross!"

"Yes... but it goes to show how people who believe in God will die for their belief. For those of you who also believe in God... would you be willing to die for your right to worship who you choose?" The class fell silent as they contemplated her question. As she collected her notes, she spoke. "If there are no more questions, you're all excused." Half the students raised their hands as excitement filled their faces. Surprised by their response, she called out with a smile. "Wow... OK." She looked around and picked the first person. "Marcy?"

As she lowered her hand, the young girl inquired. "Professor Storm... all of us are dying to know if you found the ancient sword you went looking for!" Around the room, smiling faces nodded in unison.

Storm walked to the window and stood looking out as she replied. "Yes, I found it, but... I wasn't able to keep it."

"Why?" someone called out.

Storm turned to face her class. "Someone stole it from me." A deep, collective moan filled the room as another hand shot up. "Yes?"

"Where did you finally find it?"

"On the north side of a hill in New York." The answer brought another wave of uplifted hands. Storm smiled again and pointed.

"Why would there be an ancient sword in New York?" The student asked.

Another then called out. "Yeah... all the Indians I've seen in John Wayne movies never used swords. They used bows and arrows."

As the class erupted in laughter, Storm nodded with a smile. "You're right, Tim, but this sword belonged to people who lived on this continent twenty-five hundred years ago. The American Indians are their decedants." She then picked another hand.

"So... where did they come from?"

"Good question, Mark!" Storm began. "They were led by God from Jerusalem and crossed the sea to what they called the Promised Land." With still more raised hands, a sudden rapping on the door window at the side of the classroom shifted Brenda's focus. Within it, Brenda saw the excited face of Byron McKnight. Byron was the sixty-year-old head of the anthropology department and Brenda Storm's boss. He was a tall, intelligent man with graying hair and one of Brenda's oldest, most trusted friends.

"Sorry guys… gotta go!" Brenda called out. "I'll see you all in the morning." She picked up her notes and added, "Read chapter twelve and be ready to discuss it." She walked to the door and disappeared.

Outside, Byron met her with a hug. "When did you get back?" He asked.

"Yesterday afternoon." Brenda said with a smile.

Before she could say anymore, Byron took her arm. "Come to my office… I have something incredible to tell you!"

"What is it?" Brenda questioned, with deep confusion etched into her face.

Byron checked both ways down the hall and began leading her away. He then whispered. "I have the most exciting news! Something you will find extremely interesting!"

"What?" Brenda began with a smile. "You know how many licks it takes to get to the center of a Tootsie Roll?" Not amused by her attempt at humor, Byron gave her a puzzled glance as he continued to lead her quickly through the deserted hall. "Slow down!" She commanded. "I can't walk this fast!"

Pulling her into his office, Byron closed the door behind them. He looked through the class window to make sure no one had followed. He then questioned. "You've done a lot of research on Amelia Earheart, have you not?"

Brenda smiled, her enthusiasm showing. "Well, yes. I've been fascinated with her life and disappearance since I was six. I don't think there's anything I don't know about her. Why?"

Looking around, he pulled her closer. "What if I were to tell you someone has found Amelia's plane… intact?"

Brenda's brow furrowed. "Where? At the bottom of the Pacific Ocean?"

Giggling, Byron answered. "No. Sitting in the middle of the desert at the base of mount Sinai!"

She stood staring for a moment and then questioned. "You're kidding right?" Byron said nothing as he shook his head. As the news sunk in, Brenda collapsed into a nearby chair. "Are they sure it's her plane?"

Excitedly, he moved a chair to sit beside her. "The Bedouin herders that found it got an identification number off the fuselage."

"Was there any… human remains?" She inquired.

Byron shook his head. "They didn't report seeing any, but they couldn't get inside to know for sure."

Storm's eyes grew narrow. "How did it get there? How did it get that far off course?" She shook her head. "I have always thought that her last known location was somewhere over the Pacific Ocean. It just doesn't make any since!"

"I know!" Byron agreed.

"Who told you about this? Could it be some kind of hoax?"

Byron drew closer and whispered. "The University has connections within the CIA They've asked us to put together a team to find out that very thing. They want to know if it's true before the information gets leaked to the press."

Brenda leaned forward, "Why would they want to keep such an amazing find a secret?"

Byron looked around in suspicion. "Because they found the plane in the desert so far-off course, they don't understand it. Things like this are associated with UFO sightings or governmental experiments gone bad. If it is truly Amelia's plane, they want to know how it got there after all these years and why, without causing a panic." He stood and made his way to his desk. "I chose you because of your extensive knowledge and interest in Earheart."

Brenda nodded as she stood. "Thanks Byron. This is the chance of a lifetime!" She smiled. "A true dream come true!"

"Well…" Byron began. "Let's just hope that this dream doesn't turn into a nightmare!"

"Why?" Brenda asked in confusion. "Are you expecting trouble?"

He picked up a file from his desk and made his way to stand before her. "The CIA believes others may try to get there before you, people who may want to exploit it for their own personal gain." He grew quieter as he continued. "This could very well end up being a dangerous assignment!" Handing the file to Brenda, he announced. "Besides yourself, I've chosen Howard Brimmer to go with you."

"Brimmer?" She questioned. "That little squirrely guy from the science department? I've always worked alone. Why him?"

Byron laughed, "Howard is a forensics expert. He's going to identify the remains if there are any to be found and answer any scientific questions that may arise on the expedition."

When she looked into the file, Brenda's brow furrowed. "Who is Jim Sutton?"

"He's going to be the team photographer. The CIA wants everything documented."

Brenda nodded. "I understand. What about this... Dr. Reese Manning?"

Byron shook his head. "We have assigned him as your project manager, but I know little about him."

Brenda looked at his picture and frowned. "Since when do I need a babysitter? Are we starting a business here or what?"

Byron chuckled. "I've been told he's the head of the Antiquities department at Yale University. That's all I know about him."

"I don't like it. I don't need someone telling me how to do my job!" Storm protested as she closed the file and handed it back.

As Byron placed his hand on her shoulder, he replied with a smile. "Don't worry, Brenda, you have a final say about what happens over there. I made sure of that." As he lowered his hand, he added. "I just think it's the CIA's way of spreading the glory of the find around a bit! They wouldn't want us taking all the credit for a find of this magnitude."

"So, when do I leave?" Brenda asked with an enthusiastic smile.

"How long will it take you to be ready?" He questioned as he placed the project file back on his desk.

Brenda smiled. "I haven't unpacked from my last trip. I'm ready to go now!"

Byron nodded. "That's what I love about you, Brenda!" He walked back to his desk and picked up the phone. "I've got a private plane waiting at the airport for you and Brimmer. Dr. Manning and Mr. Sutton will meet you in Egypt." Brenda sneezed and wiped her nose as Byron laughed, "Oh, and try not to take that with you!"

• • • •

Eight Years Earlier

Brenda Storm sat in the passenger's seat of her SUV as her husband Michael drove back home from a family evening out. She had met Michael while still in high school and, against their parents' wishes, had married young. He had made her extremely happy, and she always loved being around him. Now, six years later, their daughter sat in the back seat licking her favorite ice cream cone. Turning in her seat, Brenda smiled.

"Is that good?"

As the ice cream dripped down her hand, Rose replied. "Yep!"

Michael smiled as he turned for just a second to see the contentment on his daughter's face. At that very second, a drunk driver veered into their lane, striking their car almost head on at seventy miles per hour. The impact that followed crushed the driver's side and sent the vehicle into a deadly roll. As it tumbled, Brenda could see the shattered glass and metal floating through the air as in slow motion. In her ears, she heard nothing as she painfully watched her daughter's favorite teddy bear bounce off what was left of the dashboard. The eerie silence was then broken as she heard Rose screaming from the back seat.

Once the battered car came to a halt, it came to rest upright on the side of the debris-laden two-lane road, the deafening silence enveloping the scene. Brenda's head throbbed intensely, and as she instinctively reached up to check, her trembling fingers grazed a warm, sticky sensation. Blood. Her heart sank. Turning towards her husband, dread consumed her. The steering wheel had snapped off, its jagged remains mercilessly embedded deep within Michael's chest. A realization hit her like a wave crashing onto the shore - he was gone. Yet, his lifeless eyes bore deeply into her, an eerie stare that pierced her soul. Tears welled up, stinging her eyes, as she spun away, overcome by grief and disbelief.

"Oh, dear God no!" she cried out in anguish when she remembered hearing her daughter's screams. She struggled to look into the back seat and, for a moment, fought against the seat belt before being able to free herself from its protective grasp. Behind the front seats, a mangled mass of metal lay before her. "Rose?" She called out as her eyes searched for any sign of her daughter's small, frail body. On what was left of the back floorboard, she observed the ripped remains of the teddy bear her daughter had named Chester.

"Rose?" she screamed again as she struggled to get out of her seat. "Where are you?" Once free, Brenda grew dizzy and, taking a step, fell to her knees upon the gasoline covered road. As she looked down, she saw one of the teddy bear's severed legs. With tears flushing her eyes at the horrible despair she was now feeling, she called out in the darkening twilight. "Oh, God... where is she?" Suddenly, in the ditch by the side of the road, she heard a faint voice.

"Mommy?" Brenda arose and stumbled to her daughter's side.

"Mommy's here!" She replied as she knelt by her small broken body.

"Mommy... I'm so cold!" Behind a river of tears, Brenda pulled Rose into her arms.

"That's better," Rose uttered with a weak smile. Strangely, other than blood trickling from the side of her small mouth, she looked unhurt. After a moment, Brenda heard the distant sound of an ambulance approaching. It surprised Brenda as Rose then lifted her arm and pointed. With a smile, she whispered. "Look... Grandma is here with us!" Brenda turned to look, but saw no one. "She wants me to go with her!" With her statement, a new flood of tears filled Brenda's eyes. Within her life, she had always believed in an afterlife and the belief was comforting to her now. "Is it OK if I go?" Rose questioned. Her eyes were misty as they connected with her mother's.

"Yes, darling..." she said in a whisper. Her heart now broken, she touched Rose's face for the last time. "You can go."

••••

At three-twenty in the morning, two weeks later, Brenda lay in the bed she had shared with her husband for over six years. Since his death, she had often felt his presence late at night within this room, and it had helped to ease the pain of her substantial loss. Tears rolled down the side of her face as she lay facing his pillow. She reached out and, pulling it into her arms, began sobbing.

"Mother?" The voice frightened Brenda, and she shot up in her bed. "Mother?" The soft voice of a girl repeated. Startled, Brenda searched the room, but saw no one.

"Who are you?" She inquired as she pulled the blankets up around her neck. "Where are you?" The room grew brighter as a figure appeared at the foot of her bed. As she watched, it grew clearer.

"Mother?" the voice repeated a third time.

"Who are you?" Brenda repeated. Now before her, stood a young woman in her mid-twenties dressed in a long, white, glowing robe. Whiter than anything Brenda had ever seen before. She saw something familiar on this girl's face, but could not remember where she had seen her before.

"It's me, mother... Rose!"

Brenda's eyes grew narrow. "What?"

"I'm Rose... your daughter!" She assured with twinkling eyes.

It filled Brenda with love and the sure knowledge that this heavenly being was the spirit of her daughter. Tears filled her eyes. "Rose?"

"Yes Mom. It's me!"

"Can I... hug you?" Brenda questioned as she rose from the bed.

"No... I cannot be touched now!" came the soft, loving response. "But we can talk for a moment!" Brenda shook her head in disbelief. "I've come to let you know that Dad and I are all right!"

"Dad?" Brenda repeated.

"Yes... he is here with me. We're both all right!"

Brenda then pronounced. "I miss you both so very much!"

Rose's eyes grew moist. "We will all be together again. I promise!" Brenda sobbed at knowing that what she had believed her whole life was true. "Dad and I will watch over you from now on." As Brenda watched, the light faded away. Rose then added. "God has promised that we will be together for all eternity!" Brenda could only nod in response. As Rose slowly disappeared, her voice faded into a whisper as she uttered her last words. "I love you, mother!" As Rose disappeared completely, darkness again engulfed the room, and Brenda's soft whisper echoed in the silence.

"And I love you Rose!"

"Who's Rose?" Howard Brimmer inquired as he sat next to Brinda on the plane to Egypt. Brimmer was a young man of twenty-six who was still living with his parents. Being awkward, he was shy and spent most of his time alone playing video games. He had short brown hair and always wore a Yankees baseball cap that he had since he was six. He wore round Harry Potter glasses and a black Sonic the Hedgehog T-shirt. "You must have been dreaming." He added as Brenda opened her eyes.

"What did you say?" Brenda asked in confusion.

"You must have been dreaming. You said you loved somebody named Rose."

"I did?" Brenda responded as she rubbed her eyes. "Sorry."

Wanting to solve a mystery, Brimmer then asked. "So… if you don't mind me asking, who is Rose?"

Brenda leaned back and closed her eyes. "She was my daughter."

Howard's brow furrowed. "Was? What happened to her?"

Sighing, she uttered. "My husband and daughter were killed in a car crash."

Pain filled his heart as he apologized. "I'm so sorry. I shouldn't have asked. It's none of my business."

Brenda opened her eyes and annoyance filled her words. "Look… we have to work together, but that doesn't mean we have to be bosom buddies. All right?" She then leaned back and closed her eyes again. "So, don't say another word to me… understand?"

"Sorry!" Howard offered.

Brenda snapped her head around to face him and stared. He mouthed the word sorry again and then zippered his mouth closed with his fingers. Shaking her head, Brenda once again closed her eyes as the plane captain's voice filled the cabin. "Please fasten your seat belts. We will arrive at the Cairo International Airport in just a few minutes."

• • • •

Cairo Egypt

Present Day

They had recruited Justin Burk as a mercenary by the US Army to fly choppers during the Gulf War. He had an excellent reputation for getting certain things done that others considered impossible. While there, Justin Burk sustained three injuries, and people regarded him as a local legend. He was an American rebel with no respect for rules or how things were supposed to be done, and as a result, he was a valuable asset to the military. He was still fit and well-tanned, and with his present long hair and headbands, he looked more like a 1960s hippy than the aggressive cowboy he indeed was.

After the war, Burk purchased two Vietnam-era Huey Iroquois helicopters and started running charter sightseeing tours throughout Egypt, often running Arab Sheiks to their oil fields. He had built quite a reputation for himself, and his services were always in high demand and at an equally high price. In his world, they considered him the king of the sky.

On this day, he was atop the chopper he had affectionately named "Samantha," securing the engine cowl after refitting her fuel lines. Both birds were sitting on the tarmac at the south end of the Cairo airport, fifty feet from his small company office. Securing the last bolt, he turned and wiped the sweat from his brow as a string of police cars approached him. He climbed down to the tarmac and made his way to meet them.

"Mr. Justin Burk?" A large mustached man in a white suit asked as he stepped from the lead car. As he wiped his hands on a towel, Burk replied.

"Yes. Can I help you?"

"My name is Yassin Feisali, and I'm with the police." Flashing a piece of paper, he continued. "We have a search warrant to examine your helicopters!" Burk angrily folded his arms as his eyes narrowed.

"Why?"

"We have received a tip that you have been smuggling drugs into this county!" Felisali pronounced.

"Drugs?" Burk spat out with defiance. "You're barking up the wrong tree, man... I don't deal in drugs!"

Feisali smiled. "We'll see about that, Mr. Burk!" He looked at a uniformed officer and pointed to Samantha. As Burk stepped back, the officer entered the rear cargo door and looked around. Turning his back to Burk, he quickly pulled out a small white bag of heroin from his shirt pocket and pretended to find it inside a duffle bag. He then spun and held it up for everyone to see.

"No way, man!" Burk cried out in anger. "He planted that in there!" As he grew more agitated, three of the officers grabbed his arms and held him. "You won't get away with this!" He screamed.

Feisali only smiled. He then looked at the officers. "Take him away." Once the car holding Burk had driven out of sight, Feisali went to his car and returned with a small briefcase. He Handed it to the police chief and then said. "Here is the money I promised you... thanks for your help!" The police chief smiled as Feisali returned to his car and drove away.

Once off the plane, Storm and Brimmer made their way to the office of Justin Burk's charter service. Upon entering, Brenda noticed three rows of empty chairs in front of a large, messy counter. Upon the walls, she could see pictures and posters of the great pyramids of Giza, the Nile River, and other tourist sites in Egypt. She then turned her attention to a young American girl behind a desk painting her fingernails. After standing at the counter for a minute, Brenda rang a small bell on the counter.

Without looking up, the girl said. "Please take a number and wait your turn!" Storm looked at Brimmer in confusion and then spun to see the empty chairs behind her. Finding the small number dispenser on the counter, she pulled out the next ticket. She shook her head in unbelief and held the number seven up for Brimmer to see. Sitting in one of the chairs, he contently smiled as he reached for a magazine.

"There's only six people ahead of us. This shouldn't take too long!"

Tearing up the ticket in disgust, Storm called out in frustration. "Excuse me!"

"I'm sorry…" the girl answered. "But I haven't called your number yet!"

"Look! I haven't got the time for this. I have an appointment to meet Justin Burk!" Storm shouted.

Still working on her nails, the girl replied calmly, without looking up. "You have to wait till it's your turn."

Finally pushed to her limits, Storm pulled out her guns from her side holsters and announced. "I have two friends here with me, and they both think it's MY turn!"

Looking up, the girl immediately stood. "You're in luck…" she said softly. "it seems to be your turn!"

"Why doesn't that surprise me!" Brimmer exclaimed with a smile.

"Mr. Burk's not here!" The counter girl explained as she slowly neared the counter with her hands up.

Whispering, Brimmer spoke. "You can put your hands down… she's not going to kill you!" He turned to Storm in confusion and then asked. "Are you?"

Raising the weapons, Storm demanded loudly. "Where is he?"

Still staring at the guns, the girl quickly replied. "We don't know… he's been missing for two days!"

Putting the guns back into their holsters, Storm then said. "He has to be here! He's scheduled to take us into the Sinai wilderness, and it's imperative that we leave today!"

"Well…" the girl began. "Unless you can fly an Iroquois, I'm afraid you're out of luck!"

Storm placed both hands on the counter and leaned forward. "Is anyone else in this city who can fly a helicopter?"

"Our insurance policy doesn't cover that!" She replied.

Storm spun and leaned back against the counter as Brimmer stepped forward and asked. "What do we do now?"

"We go meet the rest of our team and figure something else out!"

"Where are we to meet them?" Brimmer inquired.

As Storm turned and headed for the door, she answered with a smile. "At my favorite place to eat in Cairo… The Hungry Camel!"

· · · ·

At the appointed time of the meeting, Storm and Brimmer sat at a table within the restaurant. The dining room was filled with locals conversing and enjoying the local cuisine. Most were Arabs dressed in full white robes to protect them from the harsh desert environment, making the American tourists and business people within the room stand out like sore thumbs.

"Do you have the creepy feeling we're being watched?" Brimmer whispered across the table. Remembering what Byron had told her, she nodded. She took a drink from her cloudy water glass and looked around. Along the side wall, three men looked out of place—each glaring in their direction. Fifteen minutes passed before Professor Manning and Jim Sutton walked into the room. Manning was a heavy-set man of forty-five with a bald head and a dark suit that hung like a shower curtain on his body. His dark eyes searched the room until they fell upon Storm. Jim Sutton was a young, thirty-five, handsome man with short brown hair and bright blue eyes. His body was firm and pressed against the sweat-soaked white dress shirt he wore. The black patch that covered his right eye made him look like a well-dressed pirate and only added to his dark, mysterious image.

"I presume you're Brenda Storm?" Manning questioned as they arrived at the table.

Brenda nodded. "That's right… and you are?" She asked as she stood.

"I'm Dr. Reese Manning, and this strapping young specimen is Jim Sutton."

"Hello." She pronounced as everyone shook hands. Brenda then added. "This is our forensic expert, Mr. Howard Brimmer."

"Nice to meet you all!" Jim Sutton replied with a single nod. Once they had all sat at the table, the waitress arrived.

"Are you all ready to order?"

Brimmer was the only one to pick up a menu. Looking at Manning, he asked. "Is food included in our expense account?"

"Yes." came his reply.

"Good! I'm starved!" Brimmer said with a smile. As the waitress stood with her notepad, he ordered. "I'll have the lamb and rice, two cheeseburgers, two orders of curry, a vanilla milkshake, and a large Coke with lots of ice!"

After writing, she then asked. "Are you sure you want nothing else?"

"No, he doesn't!" Manning replied with a laugh. "He just used up the food budget for five people for the entire trip!"

Brimmer looked sheepish and smiled. "This might be the last proper meal we get for months!"

Brenda was the only other person to order. "Just bring me a couple of dates and goat cheese orders. Thanks." The waitress nodded and quickly disappeared into the kitchen.

"We're already in trouble!" Brenda announced as she leaned back in her chair. "As of this second, we have no transportation!"

"What happened to our choppers?" Jim inquired as he leaned forward.

Brenda shook her head. "The pilot disappeared two days ago. We'll have to secure other means."

"That won't be easy!" Manning began. "This is prime tourist season. Everything gets booked up months in advance here! It's an extensive business!"

Brimmer then asked. "What are our other options?"

Lifting his glass of water, Manning inspected it and set it back on the table before responding. "I only know of two other choices: land cruisers or… camels!"

Brenda exhaled deeply and shook her head. "I hate camels!"

"Why?" Brimmer asked.

"I had... a bad... experience!" Storm answered with disgust in her voice.

Jim looked at her and laughed. "I don't see us having much of a choice now." The waitress returned with the food and placed it on the table. As the team ate, a large Arab man in a dirty white suit walked up to their table and stood staring in silence.

Not looking up, Brenda pronounced. "Hasn't anyone ever told you it's impolite to watch someone eat?"

"Brenda Storm?" The stranger asked.

"Yes..." she responded. "The last time I checked!" She then looked up at his face for the first time. "Can I help you with something?"

Stepping to the next table, the stranger pushed a man from his chair and pulled it next to Brenda. Sitting down, he said. "My name is Yassin Feisali."

"If that's suposta, impress me... It didn't!" Everyone except Storm stopped eating being focused on the heated conversation beginning to take place at their table.

"I'm here to tell you to return to America or be prepared to face the consequences!"

Brenda turned to look him in the eyes and replied. "And if I don't, is someone going to beat me with the same ugly stick that your mother used on you?"

Feisali laughed. "You're quite brave for a useless, female, heathen pig!" He slowly reached under the tablecloth and placed his hand high on Brenda's leg. "In my country, we have a tradition. The only thing women like you are good for is to bring joy to superior men like me!" Growing angry, Jim rose from the table in Brenda's defense. Brenda immediately grabbed his arm as he stood and pulled him back into his chair.

"Thanks, Mr. Sutton, but I can handle this myself!" Storm turned to face Feisali and, in her sexiest voice, said. "And in my county, we also have a tradition." She reached up and caressed the side of his face. "I can do something to you that you will remember for the rest of your life!" She leaned forward and whispered into his ear. "And when it's done in a public place like this... it heightens the experience!" Feisali smiled. Pulling back, Storm then asked. "But it takes a real superior man like yourself to take it. So, are you ready?"

Feisali nodded as sweat formed on his upper lip. "Yes... do it!"

Storm turned to look into Jim's confused face and then winked. Within a heartbeat and with the power of a sledgehammer, she threw her right arm backward and slammed Feisali's face with the back of her fist. For only a moment, his body sat motionless and then slowly fell forward. With a loud crack, his face slammed into Storm's goat cheese plate and remained there. The room fell silent as everyone turned to see where the sound had come from.

"Sorry!" Brenda called out to the watching crowd. "My friend here has a terrible sleeping disorder!" Without a second thought, everyone nodded their understanding and returned to their conversations. The three men against the wall immediately pulled out their daggers and began walking toward the table. When seeing them approaching, Storm stood. She pulled out a handful of cash and threw it at the table.

"Time to be going, boys!"

"What?" Brimmer cried out with a mouthful of food. "I'm not done yet!" As she pulled him away from the table, he pleaded.

"Can I at least get a doggy bag?"

Storm's eyes grew narrow. "Let's go now!" Outside, the group ran through the crowded streets of Cairo, with three thugs following in close pursuit. With pandemonium and chaos spreading within the market square, hundreds of people screamed in American, Arabic, Hebrew, and a dozen other languages. Storm began pulling over fruit-filled carts and stands to slow down the white-robbed assassins. Pushing people aside, the team rounded a corner and saw a young Bedouin boy holding a curtain open at a large stone archway.

"Here!" he yelled. "Here, you will be safe!" Without thinking, the group turned sharply and ran through the opening. After the curtain closed behind them, dozens of robed men and women carrying tables and chairs spilled out into the street. Positioned just ahead of the grand archway, the bustling crowd quickly engulfed them, their animated chatter blending with the surrounding commotion. Voices murmured in the air, occasionally interrupted by bursts of laughter. The scent of perfume and cologne mingled with the faint aroma of freshly brewed coffee, creating an intoxicating fragrance that lingered in the atmosphere. The sensation of bodies brushing against each other and the warmth radiating from the tightly packed crowd added to the illusion of genuine conversations taking place. Storm and her team were nowhere to be seen as the assassins came around the corner. Within the hallway, the group stood before the boy, trying to catch their breath. He stuck out his hand to Storm and spoke.

"My name is Yadin Hemish." Yadin was a sixteen-year-old boy who had lived alone on the streets of Cairo his whole life. Half Bedouin, half Cherokee Indian, he was obsessed with the band called The Beatles. Besides a nomad's traditional headdress and robes, he wore a black T-shirt brandishing a lime green peace sign and black high-top tennis shoes.

"I'm at your service!"

Peeking out through the curtain to the street, Manning smiled. "I'm impressed. That was quite an accomplishment!"

"All in a day's work!" Yadin replied with a smile.

Storm's eyes narrowed. "How old are you, anyway?"

"Old enough to know you need my services!"

"Your services?" Jim questioned as he stepped forward. "What might those be?"

Yadin smiled. "You're going to need camels if you're going to get to Amelia Earheart's plane!"

Storm pushed her way to the front and questioned. "How on earth did you know about that? It's suposta be a secret!"

Yadin folded his arms and smiled. "It's my job to know everything that happens in my desert. That's how I make my living!"

Manning then questioned. "So… what is it exactly that you do?"

Holding his arms out to his sides, he proudly announced. "I'm the best tour guide in all of Egypt. There is no place I can't get you to, even Earheart's plane!"

"We're still assessing our options!" Manning replied.

"Sorry..." Yadin said. "You've just run out of options. I'm your only choice."

Jim then responded. "How do you figure that?"

"There are two excellent reasons for that. To begin with, every other option is already booked for the summer. Additionally, if Feisali and his Blue Meanies are tracking you, no one else will be willing to provide transportation!"

Brimmer shook his head in confusion. "Blue Meanies?"

"You know..." Yadin began. "Bad guys, thugs, assassins... geese! Have you never seen the Beatles' movie, Yellow Submarine?" Brimmer shook his head. Yadin's voice rose in disbelief. "Man... have you lived under a rock your whole life?"

Storm smiled. "No, in his mother's basement!"

Yadin chuckled. "Awww... that explains it!"

"Hey..." Brimmer exclaimed. "I'm no mooch. I pay her twenty bucks a month for rent!"

"We would need seven camels. Five for us and two to carry our tents, equipment, and enough food and water to get us to Mount Sinai and back." Manning pronounced.

"Got it covered." Yadin happily replied.

Manning smiled. "Really?"

"Sure, no problem." He instantly shot back. "Put yourselves in my hands, and I'll take you on the best magical mystery tour you could ever request!"

"All right..." Manning said. "If we were to take you up on your offer, how much would it set us back?"

Yadin thought for a moment and then replied. "Five grand in American money!"

Storm then replied. "What? Five grand? That's crazy!"

Yadin folded his arms. "Take it or leave it. It's up to you!"

"OK, here's the deal," Manning said. "I'll pay you two thousand, and that's my last offer."

Not skipping a beat, Yadin spun and began walking away. "Have fun finding a ride!"

Storm reached out and grabbed Yadin's arm. "Alright, alright... We'll pay you five!" Looking at Manning, she added. "We don't have the time to go window shopping!"

Manning spun to face her, his eyes blazing with anger. "We're not paying some snott-nosed kid five grand Storm! And that's final!"

Brenda spun and, grabbing his lapels, threw Manning backward against the stone wall. Stepping to within inches, she spoke in a cold, lifeless voice. "We must do whatever it takes to get to that plane first... do you understand?"

"Well, I..." Manning began.

Storm then pushed him back against the wall again. "Do you understand?"

Nodding, he replied. "Yeah, I understand."

"Good!" Then, letting go, she turned and walked back through the curtain to the street. "I really hate camels!"

••••

Within the Footsteps of The Exodus

Miami Florida
June 1, 1937

On the morning of June 1, 1937, thirty-nine-year-old aviation pioneer Amelia Earheart and her husband George P. Putnam sat in a small restaurant in Miami, Florida, waiting for the server to bring them their second cup of coffee. Three miles away, Amelia's twin engine Lockheed 10-E sat on the runway. Within the cockpit, her navigator, Fred Noonan, diligently checked his charts for the third time to prepare for their journey. This journey would earn Amelia the distinction of being the first female to complete a circumnavigational flight around the world.

Amelia, a slender woman with close-cropped hair, exuded an unwavering sense of adventure. At nine years old, she embarked on her inaugural flight, courtesy of her uncle, on a makeshift roller coaster affixed to the rooftop of their family's toolshed. As the rickety wooden contraption careened off the track, she tasted the metallic tang of a bruised lip. Yet amidst the adrenaline rush, an overwhelming exhilaration coursed through her veins, solidifying her passion for the skies.

"Have I ever told you how proud I am of you?" George pronounced as he lovingly took Amelia's hand in his.

She laughed softly. "At least a million times."

"I can't help it darling… It's true!"

"You're such the example to all the other female aviators in the world!"

"All six of us?" She responded with a playful grin.

George smiled. "Six, or six thousand… it's just important that you're making a difference in the world. You help people realize women can do whatever a man can do. Sometimes even better!"

Amelia shook her head. "That will be the day!"

"It will happen Amelia... you wait and see. One day there will be women lawyers, doctors and even Police Women." He reached up and proudly touched her cheek. "And you are leading the way!" After kissing her hand, George inquired. "Is everything ready at the airport?" The waitress returned and filled their cups.

As Amelia lifted hers to her lips, she replied. "Yes. Fred is already there. We can go!"

Growing serious, George looked into Amelia's eyes. "After what happened at Luke's Field, I'm a bit nervous about this flight. It could be a bad sign." His eyes narrowed. "I just don't have a good feeling about this one."

Putting her cup down, Amelia smiled. "You getting superstitious, GP?"

He sat in silence for a moment before speaking. "I couldn't go on if anything ever happened to you!"

With a chuckle, she pronounced. "If I didn't die when I was nine, I'm never going to die!" Amelia scooted closer and kissed his cheek. "I'm going to miss you, sweetheart!"

"And I you!" George said as he kissed her back.

Amelia grew quiet and looked deeply into his eyes. "I'll be back before you know it. I promise!"

"Well..." George began. "Be sure that you do. Otherwise, I'll have no one to do my laundry!"

Amelia pulled back and playfully slapped his arm. "You wish!" She shot back with a grin. "Call Eleanor Roosevelt, maybe you can get her to do it! She owes me a favor." Both laughed as the waitress walked by. Amelia then asked. "How much do we owe you for breakfast?"

Stopping, the waitress smiled. "Nothing Miss Earheart, it's free." She took a step forward. "It's an honor to have you in our establishment. You've been such a good example to me!".

"Thank you!" Amelia replied. "I'm very grateful"

As the waitress walked away, George bragged. "See... I told you so!"

••••

"This must be the place!" Jim exclaimed, his voice echoing through the group as they approached a small business office on the outskirts of Cairo. The pungent odor of camel dung hung thickly in the air, assaulting their nostrils. Above the weathered wooden door, a crudely painted sign caught their attention - 'Abbey Road Charter Tours.' Stepping inside, they focused their attention on Yadin, who stood behind the counter. Storm scanned the room and the unexpected sight of Beatles posters mingling with images of iconic tourist attractions took her aback. And there, on the counter, sat a vintage 1960s lava lamp, its psychedelic liquid casting a mesmerizing glow, adorned with the painted faces of John, George, Paul, and Ringo.

"Welcome to my humble business. Shall we go outside and pack up?" Yadin asked as he moved from behind the counter to join them. "You brought your equipment, did you not?"

"Yes." Manning acknowledged. "It's all outside."

"Good, let's go!" Once outside, Yadin led them to the back of the building where camels sat waiting. The camels, their humps swaying in the scorching breeze, sat arranged in a neat line on the sandy ground. Vibrant yellow and red banner flags fluttered above them, reminiscent of those seen in a bustling used car lot. Yadin stood before the camels with a sense of pride emanating from him. With a smile, he turned to Brenda and said, "Since you don't fancy camels much, why don't you be the first to choose the one you want to ride?" As the team observed from a distance, Brenda strolled down the line, examining each camel carefully. When she reached the fifth one, it emitted a guttural sound and unexpectedly spat on her shirt. Disgusted, Brenda stared at the offensive stain for a moment before lifting her gaze. She summoned all her strength and delivered a forceful punch to the side of the camel's snout. The impact was immediate, causing the camel to collapse unconscious onto its side.

"I'll take this one!' Storm called out with a smile.

"Her name is Yoko..." Yadin announced. "She's a troublemaker, but she's also the most reliable I have. She's a pleasant ride!" He walked to the side of the camel next to her and pronounced. "John here is the only other camel she gets along with, so we try to keep them together!"

"I'll take him!" Jim announced.

"John, Yoko, Abby Road?" Manning asked with a smile. "Is your entire business tied to The Beatles in some way?"

"Of course! What better model could I use?" Yadin announced. "The Beatles were the ultimate band of all time. How could I go wrong with that?"

Laughing, Jim walked to Brenda's side. "I know what she did was gross, but do you really think it was necessary to punch out your camel?"

"Well..." Brenda began, "She'll think twice about spitting on me again!"

• • • •

In the cabana next to the pool at the Cairo Marriott Hotel, Feisali lifted his third glass of ice tea and took a sip. Waiting for over an hour to meet with his employer, he had become restless. Feisali had enjoyed the view of the beautiful women around him and the attention he had received by the staff of the largest hotel in Cairo, but now had grown board. He exhaled and set his glass down on the small round table before him.

Dr. Sigman Foster inquired as he approached the table. "Enjoying yourself?" He sat next to Feisali and pulled out a white cloth to wipe the sweat from his brow. "Did you warn Storm?"

Feisali's brow furrowed. "Yes, but I believe it did no good."

"Well," Foster began. "I was told you were the best in Cairo at … convincing people!"

"I am!" he refuted.

Foster picked up Feisali's glass and finished it. He slammed the empty drink upon the tabletop, smashing the glass and the top of the table into a thousand pieces. Foster glared into his eyes and questioned.

"Then what happened?" His eyes narrowed. "I'm not paying you to fail!"

"She took me by surprise… it won't happen again!" Feisali promised with pure contempt.

Foster nodded. "See that it doesn't! Storm has to be stopped at any coast!" He reached out and jabbed his finger into Feisali's chest. "Storm is not to reach that plane… do I make myself perfectly clear?"

"Yes! I have a personal score to settle with Brenda Storm!" Feisali responded in anger.

"Good." Foster began. "That's what I like to hear, my friend." As he stood, he dabbed at his forehead. "Make sure you keep me informed." An evil smile suddenly crept to his face. "If Storm should fall prey to one of the desert's many dangers, I wouldn't complain. That lass has been a problem for me for way too many years!"

• • • •

Once entering the Sinai Peninsula, the Storm caravan turned south. And according to Yadin, began following the path of the great exodus of Moses and the children of Israel. The journey was proving slow, but steadily moved toward their final destination.

"I'm still hungry!" Brimmer complained as the camel named George slowly pulled him beside Storm's.

After Shaking her head in shock, she looked over. "We had breakfast an hour ago!"

"I really don't consider dates and walnuts a balanced meal." He Adjusted his headgear and scoffed. "Where's the bacon and eggs, the pancakes, the French toast?"

"French toast?" Yadin repeated in confusion as he rode nearby.

Manning moved up beside Brimmer. "It's over two hundred and twenty miles each way to Mount Sinai and back, which means over twenty days of travel by camel. I'm afraid that limits the amount of food and water we can bring with us!" He snapped the reins, pushing his camel into a slow trot, and pulled ahead. "Sorry if we weren't able to bring along a waffle iron!"

Brenda and Jim looked on as Yadin began fumbling within his rucksack hanging from his camel's back. Pulling out an old MP3 player, he scanned its screen and pushed play. Calling out, he announced. "I thought you all would appreciate a little traveling music to pass the time. I think this song best describes our journey well." The Beatles song 'The Long and Winding Road' began playing through two large portable speakers that hung from his camel's back. The music rang out across the great expanse before them and brought a strange peace to Brenda's mind. More of an Eagles fan, she found that she could still enjoy the familiar melody she had heard a thousand times in her lifetime.

"So why did Byron McKnight choose you to head up this little joy ride of ours?" Jim inquired as he rode closer to Brenda. "I mean, besides the fact that you can knock out a camel with one punch... which is pretty impressive!"

"You're never going to let me live that down, are you?" Brenda said with a chuckle.

Jim shook his head. "Oh, no way! That minor feat is going to become part of the legend that is Brenda Storm!"

She looked into his eyes and reacted. "Gee, thanks a lot!"

"Don't mention it." He began. "It's all part of my job description."

"Do you know Byron personally?" Brenda asked after cocking her head to one side.

"No. Just read his file after they picked me to come along."

"So... who picked you?" The question took Jim by surprise.

"I umm..." he began. "Someone in the CIA recommended me,"

Brenda responded. "Friends in high places?"

Jim forced a smile. "Yea, you could say that!"

"How long have you been a photographer?"

"A while."

After she rode in silence for a moment, Brenda looked ahead. "I'm a professor of anthropology at Princeton. I've done extensive field work for Byron, and I guess I've always been interested in Amelia

Earheart and her disappearance since I was a kid. Byron knew that, so that's why he chose me... I guess."

As their camels trudged along through the deep sand, Jim Pronounced. "All I know is that she disappeared trying to fly around the world and no trace of her or her plane has ever been found." He shook his head. "I know nothing else about her."

Brenda jumped at the chance to share the story she loved so much. "In 1937, Amelia was attempting to be the first woman to fly around the world. Her and her navigator named Fred Noonan were flying a Lockheed Electra and disappeared over the Central Pacific Ocean near an island called Howland." As she spoke, her eyes brightened with excitement. "The last radio message they sent said they couldn't find the island, and they were running low on fuel."

Jim's brow furrowed. "The Central Pacific Ocean?" He looked at Brenda and shook his head in confusion. "If they were that low on fuel, there is no way they could have made it all the way to the Sinai Peninsula!"

Brenda stopped her camel and focused intently on Jim. "Exactly! That's the mystery we're here to solve!"

"After they disappeared, didn't they look for them?"

"Yeah, extensively... an hour after Earheart's last message, a coast guard ship called the Itasca began a search around the island they were scheduled to land on to refuel, but nothing was ever found. Four days later, on July sixth, a US battleship called the Colorado was called in to take over the search." Brenda looked at the horizon and spoke softer. "They found no sign of them or the plane."

"Seems to me..." Jim Began with a smile. "If they were able to find the Titanic, they should have been able to find her plane!"

"The same guy that found the Titanic searched for it as well, but came up with nothing." Brenda explained. "It's almost like it disappeared off the face of the earth..."

"And amidst the vast expanse of the Sinai Desert, it materialized without a single scratch after all these years," Jim recounted, his voice carrying a sense of awe. As he turned to meet her gaze, a soft breeze brushed against his skin, the sand beneath his camel's feet shifting like a gentle whisper. At that moment, Brenda's breathtaking beauty captivated him for the first time, his heart soaring with unexpected delight. Attempting to shake off these unanticipated emotions, he shook his head, seeking to dislodge the overwhelming feelings that had taken hold of him.

"I'm glad they picked me for this expedition!" He pronounced in his effort to divert his attention.

Confusion filled Brenda's face as she looked ahead. "I was going to ask you about that. You've been wearing that Nikon around your neck since we first met, but I've never seen you take a single picture." She turned and laughed. "Did you forget your film?"

He explained. "They hired me to document Earheart's' plane if it's really there. Nothing more!"

Brenda's brow furrowed. "Nothing to get bent outa shape about, I just thought it was a bit strange."

Growing nervous, Jim replied in defense. "What? Do you think I can't control myself from taking pictures of the most beautiful woman I've ever seen?"

"What did you just say?"

Amazed at what he had blurted out, he looked to the horizon. Then, in a panic, he replied. "Well, think again, girly. You don't affect me in the least!" His attempt to hide his feelings for Brenda had the opposite effect,

"Excuse me?" Brenda began. "I was not trying to... effect you at all!!" She turned from his view and added. "If I have... that's your problem, not mine." Lying, she continued. "I could never be interested in someone like you!"

"Fine!" Jim spat out.

"Fine!" Brenda repeated with the same fury that he had given her. She kicked at Yoko's flanks and snapped her reins. "Chee, Chee, Chee!" she called out, bringing her camel to a brisk run. Being left in the dust, Jim sat shaking his head at his own stupidity.

· · · ·

Fortaleza, Brazil

June 4, 1937

In July 1936, Purdue University financed the building of the Lockheed 10-E that Amelia Earheart now found herself flying in as she headed from Paramaribo, Surinam, to Fortaleza, Brazil, on the first leg of her around-the-world flight. The plane included extensive modifications, including six extra fuel tanks, bringing a total capacity to one thousand, one hundred fifty-one gallons. With only one hundred-forty-nine made, the Model 10 Electra was a twin-engine plane with a wingspan of fifty-five feet and a cruising speed of one hundred seventy-five miles per hour. In 1937, it was one of the most advanced aircraft of its time.

Amelia now sat in the pilot's seat, fighting to keep the plane level as it flew through turbulent storm clouds. She finished checking her airspeed and oil pressure gauges upon the control panel before her and reached down, pushing the two main throttle controls forward, and took the plane to a higher altitude to get above the Storm. After Fred Noonan's trip to the bathroom stall in the aircraft's rear, his head appeared within the cabin as he climbed over the fuel tanks.

"I swear that if I throw up one more time…" He announced as he took his appointed seat next to Amelia.

Pulling the radio headset from her ears, she laughed. "What's the matter, Fred? Aren't you used to this by now?"

He looked over and spoke. "It's you're flying that's making me sick. Maybe you should try taking some flying lessons!" At that second, the plane suddenly lurched in the turbulence. Fred's face turned white as he braced himself in the cabin.

Smiling, Amelia questioned. "Do you subscribe to the existence of God?

He shifted his position to face her. "No, not really… why?"

Amelia announced. "This might be a good time to start!" When the altitude gauge rose to seventeen thousand feet, she leveled the plane off and looked at Fred. "Do you believe we evolved from monkeys?"

"What?"

"Just answer the question... yes or no."

Fred looked out the cabin window a moment and responded. "I guess. That's what some people believe."

"If that's true..." Amelia argued. "Why are there still monkeys?"

Fred's eyebrows arched. "Never thought of that before."

Amelia added. "The same people who tell us that are the same ones who tell us a woman can't do the same things men can do!"

Fred shook his head with a smile. "Let's not go beating that dead horse again today!"

"Sorry!" Amelia began. "I'm just passionate about that subject!"

Fred nodded. "Yeah, tell me about it!"

"God is real, Fred... in that, I know!" Amelia testified with deep conviction. "If we accept his gospel and keep the commandments, we can have eternal life!"

Fred turned to face her. "Wow... maybe you should have been a preacher instead of an aviator!"

"Sorry!" she apologized again. "Passionate about that as well!"

Fred said with a smile. "I don't think there's anything you're not passionate about! It's just who you are."

Amelia nodded and replaced her headset. Tuning in the radio, she contacted the Fortaleza Airport.

"This is KHAQQ approaching at seven thousand feet. Requesting permission to land. Over."

"KHAQQ..." A voice crackled in her ears. "This is Fortaleza Airport. You have permission to land your aircraft. Over. Please approach from the North East. Over."

• • • •

The end of each day's journey within the wilderness was almost always the same. When dusk settled upon the caravan, they stopped to make camp. Someone would bring together and hobble the camels, which prevented them from wandering off at night. Sitting together in a line on the sand, they rested from their duties. The team would set up colorful one-person tents in a semi-circle around the area designated for food preparation and where they could congregate for the evening. In the center of all was a small single-flame propane burner used to heat their food or water, providing minimal heat on the cold evenings.

On this night, the stars above them shone like a million tiny candles within the vastness of a field of black velvet. The moon was full and bright and seemed more prominent than usual as it sat above the horizon.

As Brenda looked up into the heavens, Yadin sat on his blanket beside her. "Now, let there be lights in the firmament of the heavens to give light upon the earth: and it was so, And God made two brilliant lights; the greater to rule the day and the lesser to rule the night; he made the stars as well."

"Amen," Brenda said as she continued to look at the night sky.

On the other side of Yadin, Jim lifted the water pot from its place upon the burner. "Anyone want any tea?"

"Yeah. I'll have some." Brenda held out her empty tin cup as Jim filled it.

Manning questioned as he drank from his cup. "So, I take it you don't like coffee? You always have tea."

Brenda placed her tea bag into her cup and responded. "Coffee's not good for you!"

"Why do you say that?"

Brenda stirred her cup and then said. "The caffeine within coffee damages your adrenal glands and breaks down important body tissues and organs. It also leaches calcium from your bones. Besides all of that..." she added, "it's addictive. I stay away from anything that could control my life and choices. I used to drink it, but I hated the depression I felt when I came down."

"Sounds like a smart idea to me," Yadin said. He leaned back on the duffle bag he had used as a pillow and added. "Doing these tours, I've seen addictions drive many people to do some stupid stuff."

"That's the truth!" Jim agreed as he pulled his tea bag from his cup.

Manning shook his head. "I don't believe a little coffee hurts anyone."

Brenda looked into her cup and briskly danced her tea bag inside it. "Would you be willing to stop drinking it from now on?"

Manning looked puzzled for a moment and then said. "No, I like it too much!" She nodded as she removed the bag from her cup. "Point proven!" Sipping from his cup of coffee, Brimmer chuckled. Brenda spun to face him. "What are you laughing at? You drink it, too!" Brenda's sudden question caught him off guard, instantly taking him aback. As he lifted his cup to his lips, he froze and stared into it. After a moment, he sat it down on the sand beside him.

"Where are we anyway?" Jim looked at the sky. Somewhere in the distance, a camel bellowed loudly.

"Ayun Musa," Yadin answered as he looked up at the moon.

"Excuse me?" Brimmer questioned with a furrowed brow.

Yadin then repeated with a smile. "Ayun Musa in the wilderness of Etham. In the days of Moses, it was called Mariah."

Brenda took a sip of her tea and quoted from the Bible. "And when they came to Mariah, they could not drink the water, for it was bitter, and the people murmured against Moses saying, what shall we drink? And he cried unto the Lord, and the Lord showed him a tree, which when it was cast into the waters, the waters were made sweet."

"Yeah, right!" Manning responded loudly. "Do you people really believe all that Moses crap?" With a hostile gesture, he shook his head.

"Documents in the Qumran and other places verify his existence and the Bible."

"Qumran? What's that?" Jim Asked.

Brenda leaned forward and set her teacup down. "They found the Dead Sea scrolls there. Qumran was where a small brotherhood of Essenes of the Monastic Order built a settlement in 160 BC. It's on the Alluvial Plateau overlooking the shores of the Dead Sea."

Manning looked at Jim and said with a laugh. "They collected religious fairy tales in clay pots. Look…" Manning added. "Fake documents are created and handed out all the time!"

"Facts, Manning, facts!" Brenda said with conviction.

"Whatever."

Brenda grew angry. "How can you claim to be a professor of antiquities and teach at Yale without believing in the truth?"

Manning turned to face her, his voice rising. "History has been happening for millions of years, and all of it can be explained without all the religious mumbo, jumbo that weak-minded people like you try to connect to it!"

Her fury growing, Brenda said. "How many thousands of young students have you corrupted with your lectures?"

"Not enough!" Manning shot back. He stood and walked away into the darkness.

Yadin sighed and continued Brenda's story. "In AD 68, the settlement was destroyed by a Roman legion, but not before someone had hidden all the scrolls in nearby caves. There, they remained undiscovered for over nineteen hundred years."

"Wow, that's quite a story!" Jim responded quietly.

"Well, what's exciting is that recently, a new scroll has been translated!" Brenda began with excitement.

Turning to look at her, Jim then asked. "What did it say?"

"Well, if you know the Bible, you probably remember that once Moses reached the Promised Land, God did not allow him to enter."

"Yeah," Jim responded. "I knew that."

Brenda's eyes grew bright, like a child's on Christmas morning. "After guiding the Children of Israel to the promised land, Moses returned to Mount Sinai, and the scroll reveals God took him to Heaven. It also says that his staff was left behind!"

Jim looked confused. "That makes sense, but... what difference does that make?"

Brenda quickly moved to her knees in the sand before him. "Don't you see? That means his staff is still there, somewhere to be found!"

Brimmer spoke up. "And you think you can find it?"

Manning suddenly appeared from the darkness and stood beside her. "Hogwash!" he yelled. "It's just a stupid fantasy story told by some madman over two thousand years ago!"

"Think what you like…" Brenda said. "But I choose to believe it!"

Manning spun and headed for his tent. "Believe what you want. I'm done talking!"

After a moment, Brimmer and Yadin both stood together. "I'm going to call it a night as well."

"Me too," Yadin said. "I think we all need to calm down a bit."

Brenda looked up into their faces. "Good night, guys." In silence, she looked at Jim, who sat beside the small fire. "You mean I haven't scared you off as well with my religious mumbo jumbo?"

Jim poured out the last bit of his tea. "Nope… can't get rid of me that easily." Listening to them talk inside his tent, Yadin smiled. He was young but had a romantic heart, even at his age. In the past, he had successfully brought strangers together on his tours, and this was just another challenge. A moment later, 'Yesterday' by the Beatles began playing softly as the soundtrack to their quiet conversation.

At hearing the music, Storm looked in Yadin's direction and smiled. "Do you think that's subtle enough?"

Yadin responded from the dark. "Just doin' my job!"

Jim looked away. "Does he think something is going on between us?"

Brenda smiled. "What a crazy idea!"

Jim looked away. "Yeah, really crazy!" Looking back at her, he continued. "So, Brenda Storm… what makes you so tough?"

"You think I'm tough? What makes you think that?"

"Well, for one thing, I've seen no one else knock out a camel with a right cross before!" Jim laughed. "Oh, and let's not forget how you handled Feisali back there."

Brenda looked at the fading horizon. "Yeah, I guess you're right."

"So, what's your story?"

Brenda sat in silence for a moment, collecting her thoughts. Her voice was low and emotional when she explained.

"My husband and daughter were killed in an auto accident, and there was nothing I could do to stop it. I felt helpless." She then looked into Jim's eyes as she struggled to continue. "It was a horrible feeling that I promised myself I would never experience again. I joined the Army and earned my way into the Special Forces, where I learned everything I could about being in control of myself and my surroundings." She then added. "The result is who you see before you. The one and only Brenda Storm, the…"

"Woman, the legend!" Jim finished her sentence with a laugh.

"Hardly!" she said.

Jim suddenly grew serious. "What was your husband's name?"

"Michael."

"What was he like?" Jim inquired.

Turning her body to face him, she questioned. "Why do you want to know?"

"Just curious. I'd really like to get to know you better."

She sat in silence as her eyes grew moist with Michael's memory. "He was the kindest man I've ever known. I didn't think loving someone as much as I loved him was possible." She shook her head. "He always made me feel like I was the center of his world."

Jim nodded. He stood and made his way to her side and sat down again. "I was almost married once," He began as he drew a heart in the sand with his finger. "She always made me feel like being wrapped in a warm blanket on a cold, rainy night."

Wiping the tears from her face, Brenda then questioned. "So, what happened?"

"She couldn't handle not knowing if I was going to come back alive every night," Jim responded without thinking.

"Why?" Storm questioned as she leaned forward. "Was she afraid you'd die in your darkroom because you couldn't find your way out?"

Jim shook his head. "No… sometimes I can get called to go out on a few dangerous assignments."

"Like military stuff?"

"Yea, Kinda." Trying to lighten the mood, Jim then said. "So… do you think there's any hope for people like us?"

"In what way?"

As Jim poured more hot water into his empty cup, he smiled. "People who don't drink coffee!"

Brenda snorted. "It's worked for me!"

He then held out his cup to her. "Have any extra tea bags?"

The sun was up at six o'clock the following morning, flooding the sand around the camp in a beautiful orange glow. With the new sun, the warmth returned to the ground. Brenda had slept outside her tent and began to stir beneath a calico wool blanket. When opening her eyes, she gasped in horror. Sitting inches before her face was a giant black scorpion, its tail poised for attack. She had never seen one this close, and the image was frightening. She slowly backed away and noticed a dozen more crawling upon her blanket.

"Jim?" she whispered as she now lay still. Fighting the urge to scream, she called out again. "Jim?" The sudden desire to vomit crept into her stomach, and she struggled to keep it down. "Is anyone there?" She asked. Yadin was the first to see her as he climbed from his tent. Seeing the danger, he ran to Jim's tent.

"Mr. Sutton… I think we might have a slight problem!"

Hearing the fear in his voice, Jim appeared at his tent opening. "What's the matter?" Not able to speak, Yadin pointed to Brenda's unmoving body. Moving closer. He called out.

"Brenda? Are you all right?"

With deep fear in her voice, she replied. "Why wouldn't I be? Doesn't everyone sleep with scorpions to keep them warm?" Moving quickly to his camel, Jim pulled out a sizeable military shotgun and returned.

"What on earth do you think you'll do with that?" Brimmer wondered as he drew near.

Taking a step closer, Jim held up the shotgun. "Whatever you do, don't move!"

Yadin walked to his side and pushed the weapon down. "That's not the way to handle this, Mr. Sutton."

Looking him in the eyes, he suggested. "I need you to build a fire… right now!"

Brimmer's brow furrowed in his confusion. "How can you be thinking about breakfast at a time like this?"

"No, not breakfast, Mr. Brimmer!" Once the fire started, Yadin found a long wooden tent stake and held one end in the flames until it ignited. Then, removing it, he held it up. "Scorpions fear fire, Mr. Brimmer," Yadin said, his voice laced with urgency. He walked cautiously towards Brenda's body, the acrid scent of smoke hanging heavy in the air. With a tight hold on the stick, he extended it towards the nearest scorpion, its dark exoskeleton glistening under the flames. As the fire inched closer, the scorpion scuttled away, its legs scraping against the wool echoing in the silence. Determined, Yadin repeated the process, removing each scorpion from harm's way.

Once the area was clear, Jim reached out a hand to help Storm up, his palm rough against her skin. Stepping back, he positioned himself, shotgun in hand, and with four precise shots, he removed the danger. He spun around to face Storm. His eyes found hers, filled with a mix of relief and determination. Without hesitation, he took her hand, their fingers intertwining like a perfect fit, creating a sense of comfort and resilience.

"Are you all right?"

Shaken, her eyes grew misty. "You handle a shotgun pretty well for a... photographer!"

"Well..." Jim began nervously. "I've had some... practice."

She forced a smile and spoke. "You'd think someone who could knock out a camel wouldn't be afraid of a few little bugs!"

Yadin's face turned somber. "That shouldn't have happened!"

Storm nodded. "You can say that again!"

"No!" Yadin explained. "You don't understand. This would never have happened in real life!" Looking at the remains, he continued. "This variety of scorpion is not indigenous to this area. There is no way they should be here at all!"

Storm's voice grew louder. "What are you saying?"

Yadin looked from face to face. "I'm saying... someone placed those scorpions on you!"

Manning took a step forward. "You mean... one of us?"

Yadin nodded his head. "Yes... that's exactly what I mean!"

••••

By late afternoon, the caravan had drifted apart more than a half mile. As usual, Yadin was far out ahead, with Storm close behind. Within her white robes that protected her from the harsh elements of the desert, Brenda caught herself sleeping for the third time in an hour. She reached down, pulled a goat's bladder filled with water from its place on Yoko's back, and took a long, refreshing drink of the warm liquid.

"Hey!" Jim's voice called out from behind her. "You mind some company?"

With a nod, she looked back. "If you can keep up." Jim's camel loudly protested as he snapped the reins and kicked at his flanks, and Trotting, it moved to Brenda's side.

"How do you feel about what Yadin said this morning?" Brenda remained aloof as Yoko moved forward. Her mind had been on nothing else for the last five hours, and it had done little to resolve the question that now occupied her thoughts. She looked at him with a coldness that had never been there before.

"What? That someone on my team might be trying to kill me? How would you feel?"

Jim's eyes narrowed. "I hope you don't believe it's me!"

Growing angry and frustrated, she instantly snapped back. "It could be!" She then shook her head sadly. "I just don't know who I can trust anymore. It's very unsettling to me!" She then turned to face the horizon. "One thing is for sure now… Someone doesn't want me reaching that plane!" Storm's voice grew cold as she turned back and stared into Jim's eyes. "And I will kill anyone who tries to stop me. Anyone!"

Up ahead of them, Yadin had stopped. Turning his animal around, he trotted back to join them. "We've got trouble!"

Brenda rolled her eyes. "Haven't we had enough for one day?"

Jim then added. "What's the problem now?"

Yadin pointed behind them. "There's a sandstorm coming!" Turning around, they stood in awe as a wall of sand at a staggering height of two hundred feet surged forward with astonishing speed. The sight was mesmerizing as the sand particles danced and swirled.

The deafening roar of the wind mixed with the faint rumbling of the shifting sand, creating a symphony of nature's power. A dry, earthy scent filled the air like the desert had come alive. The sheer force of the sandstorm sent a tingling sensation down their spines, reminding them of the immense energy contained within the natural phenomenon.

"If we don't make cover... we'll all die!"

"Where on earth are we going to find cover out here?" Brenda called out with trepidation creeping into her voice.

Dismounting, Yadin pronounced. "We brought our own."

"What?" Jim cried. "What are you talking about?"

"We've got to get the tents off the pack animals." Yadin placed his fingers into his mouth and whistled. Manning and Brimmer rode up with the pack animals in tow within a few minutes. As the sandstorm grew closer, Yadin screamed. "Get the tents out now!"

"What's going on?" Brimmer asked. Brenda then pointed.

"You've got to be kidding me!" He called out in horror.

"Hurry... now!" Yadin repeated. Once unloaded, he then commanded. "Now get the camels in a circle with their heads together, cover them with the biggest tent, and climb under with them!"

"Are you crazy?" Brimmer screamed.

Yadin spun to face him. "If you stay out here, the sand will tear the skin from your body, and you will die, anyway!" As he moved toward the tent, he added. "But I suggest you decide now!" At the last second, Brimmer crawled under and joined the rest of the team just as the sandstorm hit. Within minutes, it buried them under a foot of sand. After a half hour of howling wind and sand, the group still lay within the air pocket that had saved their lives. One camel bellowed loudly.

"What's that putrid smell?" Brimmer called out, his voice echoing in the pitch-black darkness. Fumbling in his pocket, he retrieved his phone and activated the flashlight app. The piercing beam revealed an animal's face in front of him, who then belched. Its smell invaded Brimmer's nostrils, triggering tears in his eyes. The overpowering stench made him almost vomit, and he somehow said. "George, you seriously need some breath mints!" The team burst into laughter, their joy cutting through the tension and bringing a sense of relief to the oppressive situation.

"He probably thinks the same thing about you!" Manning said with a smile.

"When will it be safe to get out from under this thing?" Brimmer asked as he pushed up on the tent canvas. "I need some fresh air!"

Yadin explained. "Well… most sandstorms don't last too long. Some have swallowed entire cities, but this one is not that big. It won't be long now!"

••••

Fort-Lamy, F.E. Africa

June 11, 1937

Eight hundred miles out of French Sudan, Amelia was within a hundred miles of her first refueling stop in Africa. Because of thick clouds, she throttled back to seventeen hundred RPM and reduced her altitude to seven hundred feet. From that point, everything seemed fine. Amelia was growing tired and hungry. Holding up two identical sandwiches, Fred looked at her and asked.

"Ham and cheese or ham and cheese?"

With a smile, she replied. "You know how bad I hate to make decisions, Fred... surprise me!" "Ham and cheese, it is then!"

Amelia laughed as she looked down between the seats. "Grab me one of those Coca-Colas, would you?" After Fred opened her bottle, he handed it to her and opened one for himself. Amelia smiled and held out her bottle to him.

"Here's to the fringe benefits of mass-market product endorsements!" Fred lifted his and tapped the two together with a laugh. With the help of her future husband George, Amelia had been successful in marketing campaigns for Lucky Strike cigarettes, a woman's clothing line, her brand of luggage named 'Modernaire Earheart Luggage,' and several other profitable endorsements. She took a small bite of her sandwich and looked into the clear blue sky ahead of them.

"Oh, Fred," Amelia exclaimed, her voice filled with awe, "Isn't this the most breathtaking sight you've ever seen?" Fred, captivated by the scene before him, nodded in agreement. "This," she replied, her voice filled with a deep sense of fulfillment, "is why I became an aviator." Amelia's voice transformed into a melodic tune as she sang. "Somewhere over the rainbow, bluebirds fly..." Her voice carried through the air, mingling with the gentle hum of the engines. Spinning around, her face illuminated with excitement, she turned towards Fred and eagerly asked,

"Did you see The Wizard of Oz?"

With another nod, Fred replied, "Yes, I believe everyone on this planet has witnessed its magic."

Taking a sip of her soda, Amelia paused and continued, "When Dorothy walks from her black and white world into the glorious colors of the land of OZ, it encapsulates how I feel every time I step into a plane and soar into the sky. It's an indescribable sensation, truly wonderful."

"Oh…" Fred called out. "Did you see Flash Gordon last year?"

Amelia's eyes grew large, her excitement growing. "Yes!" she called out. "Six times!"

Laughing, Fred replied. "I thought you would have liked that one!"

"Do you blame me? The whole idea of space travel is unbelievable. If possible, I'd want to be the first woman on the moon!"

"Or Mars!" Fred added.

"Exactly!" She giggled like a small child.

Fred then smiled. "I'll let you go if you promise to take me with you. You'll need a navigator!"

"Deal!" Amelia replied. At that moment, the plane shuddered.

"What was that?" Fred asked as he looked through the crawlspace to the back. Amelia's face grew serious as she looked at the gauges above her head.

She called out as she looked out both side cabin windows to check the engines. "Something doesn't feel right." she looked down before her and tapped on the oil pressure gauge for the left Pratt and Whitney engine. After the tap, the pressure dropped to a dangerously low level. "We've got a problem!"

"What is it?" Fred inquired.

"We've got low oil pressure in the left engine." Fred fastened his seat belt and turned to Amelia.

"I think we can make it. I'll throttle back and monitor the engine."

"And if we can't?" Fred asked coldly.

"Well, if the engine blows, we'll just have to land and hope we don't hit an elephant!" She said with a laugh.

Fred grabbed the sides of his seat and closed his eyes. "If that was suposta be funny… It wasn't!"

••••

Nahal Haheeb

After a long day of travel, Storm eased herself down by the fire as she meticulously combed through her belongings, desperately searching for the map of the Mount Sinai region. A slight chill had settled in as the darkness drew upon the camp, making her uncomfortable. She reached out and placed her hands above the small fire and smiled.

Manning was within his tent, searching through his three duffle bags for his coffee cup, and Brimmer was securing the camels for the night—an unwelcome task in the camp. As Jim and Yadin approached, Brenda looked up and asked.

"How much further is it to Saint Catherine?"

Yadin replied. "We are about halfway there." As he sat between her and Sutton, he then asked. "Why?"

Looking back at the map, she explained. "Our contact is there. The only one who can lead us to the plane."

"If I had known you wanted to go there, I would have charged you more."

"Why's that?" Storm inquired.

"It's a dangerous place, Miss Storm! Too dangerous for tourists!"

Jim then looked at Yadin. "Why?"

"A cult has existed in those lands for over five thousand years. They were followers of a Mesopotamian moon God called Sin. He is also called Manna, Asimbabbar, Namrasit, and Inbu."

"Are they still around?" Jim asked in surprise.

"Yes, I'm afraid so," Yadin said. "And very much still active!"

"Who is this… Sin guy?" Jim inquired.

Brenda then turned to him. "In Mesopotamian mythology, Ereshigal was the queen of the dead. She ruled the underworld, and Sin played the role of judge of the dead. He decreed their fate."

"So, what's that got to do with this Saint Catherine place?" He questioned.

Yadin then answered. "Saint Catherine is at the base of Mount Sinai, and it's said that there is an ancient sanctuary of Sin nearby." Yadin shook his head. "Some say cult members dwell within the city and still perform human sacrifice."

"Well… I can see why you think it's a terrible place!" Jim said.

Yadin's face grew bitter. "We should not venture into such an evil place." Behind them, two camels bellowed as Yadin warmed his hands.

"If you are bound and determined to go there, we must be vigilant."

As Brenda nodded, the camels grew louder. "What in the world are they so upset about?" She asked as she turned in their direction.

Out of the darkness, Brimmer neared them and stopped with a look of fear etched upon his face. He looked back over his shoulder and spoke.

"Someone's out there!" The distant sound of snorting horses reverberated through the crisp night air. With wide eyes, the group spun around, their gazes fixed on the shadows beyond the fire. Their astonishment grew as four riders cloaked in billowing white robes, adorned with a vibrant red sash, and veiled to conceal their identities emerged from the darkness astride majestic black Arabian stallions. The riders exuded an air of mystery. The flickering torches gripped tightly by the outermost riders cast an ethereal glow, illuminating their path. Adorned on their large white banners was a simple symbol—a fish- symbolizing a Christian connection. The two riders at the center gracefully dismounted and stepped into the warm embrace of the fire's light, positioning themselves before the group.

Sensing the tension, Storm's hand inched towards her holstered guns while Yadin's voice escaped his lips as a whisper. "Put your weapons away. You won't be needing them."

As she did so, the tallest rider pulled the veil from his face. "Why do you seek Jebel Musa?… The Mountain of Moses?"

Jim took a step forward and asked. "Why are you here, and what concern are we to you?"

Yadin then whispered from behind. "Careful, Mr. Sutton. You don't know who you are talking to!"

"Who is he?" Jim whispered back.

"He is a man of God... a prophet to these people."

"My name is Jehorum..." the man began. He then looked out into the darkness and raised his arms. "And we are the Guardians of the Exodus!"

Brimmer laughed. "Sounds like an Indiana Jones movie title."

Brenda whispered. "Unless you're trying to get yourself killed, I'd suggest you keep quiet!" She then stepped forward. "My name is Brenda Storm, and I oversee this expedition. We are only here seeking a lost airplane that sits somewhere at the base of Mount Sinai." As she studied the second rider, she concluded it was a girl. Jehorum turned to her, and something unspoken passed between them.

"We are servants of our Savior Jesus Christ and have been called to protect the antiquities of God's hand among the children of Israel during the Great Exodus." Jehorum then said. "They have handed us this great privilege from father to son for over two thousand years."

"Did someone say antiquities?" Manning inquired as he made his way out of the darkness to stand beside Storm.

"Don't get any ideas!" Brenda called out softly.

"What antiquities are we talking about, my friend?"

"Manning..." Brenda threatened.

He turned to her and smiled. "What? I'm just asking!"

Jehorum took a step forward. "Sacred treasures that the Lord does not want in the hands of mortals!"

Manning smiled. "Such as..."

"Manning... don't even think about it!" Storm said.

"Onyx stones and precious gems, shittimwood overlayed with pure gold used in the tabernacle's creation that held the ark of the testimony. The ark itself with its golden cherubim, the mercy seat, and crowns. The sacred staff of Moses and the serpent created by

Aaron to heal the children of Israel and many more, all held within the safety of the earth until the Lord sees fit for their discovery."

"You know…" Manning began. "If the Lord wants them discovered, I could take care of that for Him!"

"Silence!" Jehorum said. Instantly, sixty-two rifles trained on him.

"OK… I guess I can take that as a no?"

Jehorum turned back to face Storm as a strange silence fell upon the camp. He stood with his eyes closed for a moment, and then, with a voice filled with compassion and touching her very soul, he said,

"Your husband, Michael, and your daughter, Rose, want you to know how much they love you!"

Tears welled up in Brenda's eyes as she replied in confusion. "How do you know about my family?"

She could feel a deep love and connection in his eyes that warmed her body from the inside out. He reached out and touched her arm. "They are here with us right now! I hear them!" He then took a step forward and embraced her. "Our brother, Jesus Christ, also wants you to know that he's caring for them until you are together again."

Brenda began sobbing as she returned his hug. She said. "Tell them I love them as well!"

Jehorum then smiled. "They can hear you!" Pulling away, he smiled again. "We must depart now," He said. The moonlight bathed the scene in a soft glow as he locked eyes with her. "I assure you, with unwavering certainty, that you will find for a moment what you seek and much more." His words hung in the night air. In one fluid motion, he spun around, his cloak billowing behind him. With his mysterious companion by his side, they mounted their horses.

"The Lord's love envelops you, Brenda Storm," he said, his voice filled with conviction. "You belong to Him, and He to you!" His words wrapped around her like a warm embrace, comforting her troubled soul. With a smile, Brenda wiped away the tears that stained her cheeks. She stood there, bidding farewell to the Guardians of the Exodus. As they departed, a serene silence enveloped the scene, interrupted only by the distant sounds of the horse's hooves upon the sand and the whisper of the wind. They faded into the velvety darkness of the night, leaving behind only a sense of majesty.

"Wow, did that just happen?" Jim asked as he walked to Brenda's side. "Are you all right?" Brenda nodded with a smile.

"If I was religious…" Jim began. "I might believe something spiritual just happened here."

"Hogwash!" Manning laughed. "It's all mumbo-jumbo!"

"If that were true, how did he know about Brenda's family?" Jim questioned.

"Are you kidding? Anyone with computer access could have found out that information. There was no miracle in what he said!"

"What? Are you out of your mind?" Brenda's brow furrowed. "I believe him. I could see it in his eyes!"

"The only thing you saw in his eyes was the peyote he's been smoking!" Manning said with a smile.

Brenda then said. "I didn't see you questioning anything he said about the antiquities he described!"

"Gold is gold… You don't have to believe in God to reap its benefits!" Manning pronounced with a smile. "Now, if you will excuse me, I have plans to make of my own!"

· · · ·

Bangkok, Siam

June 20, 1937

As usual, upon landing, Amelia and Fred saw to the re-fueling and supplies needed for the next leg of their flight. Engines were being checked, fluids filled, radio equipment maintained and enough food, snacks and beverages to keep them happy until they reached their next destination. Any prior problems they experienced during the previous flight became top priority. Once done, a man in a long, black trench coat approached Amelia and Fred.

"My name is John Thornton. It's an honor to be in your presence."

Fred moved forward and shook his hand. "Why thank you Mr. Thornton. We're glad to be here.!"

As Amelia shook his hand, she inquired. "You're American?"

Thornton smiled as he replied. "Yes, born in New York but I've got... business partners here.! I'm a big fan of yours and wanted to meet you!"

"Wow!" Amelia laughed as she looked at Fred. "Never expected that." Thornton then said with a smile. "I would like to offer you a place to freshen up from your journey before you continue with your flight!" Amelia looked at her watch. "That would be nice. We have a few hours to spare before we have to go." Looking at Fred, she asked. "What do you think?"

"Sounds good to me. I could use a shower and some proper food!"

Staying in the best suite in the Bangkok Hilton, Amelia held the phone to her ear as she walked to the couch.

"Oh, George... I miss you so much!"

Her husband then replied from America. "And I miss you Sweetums!"

"George!" Amelia called out. "You know how much I hate it when you call me that!"

"Sorry!" He replied.

As she sat herself down, she smiled. "I wish you could be here with me. It's all so exciting!"

George then asked. "So, where are you today?"

"Bangkok!" she cried out in great excitement. "Going to all these exotic places is wonderful, but we don't have time to see much from the ground."

"When you get home, well go back together." George said with a smile. At that moment, someone knocked on the door.

"George?" she began. "I believe someone is at my door. I'm going to go now."

"It's probably a reporter!" He said. "OK dear, I love you!" Amelia put the phone on the table and checked her short-cropped hair in a mirror. Because she knew that her hair was naturally messy looking anyway, she laughed to herself as she opened the door.

"Fred?" She cried out. "Miss me all ready?"

"Couldn't keep myself away from you!" He replied as he stepped into the richly decorated suite. Looking around, he added. "This is really nice!" A moment later, he turned to face her. "They put me in a broom closet!" Amelia laughed. "They did not!"

"Well…" he said. "Almost!" As they sat together on the forest green couch, Fred found Amelia's eyes. "So, have you called GP yet?"

"Yes." She answered. "Just got off the phone with him!"

With a mischievous grin, he then asked. "Did you finally tell him you're leaving him for me?"

Amelia laughed. "No… not yet!"

Fred then grew serious. "I can't believe you married anyone. It just doesn't fit your free spirit!"

Amelia began pouring water into a glass as she replied. "I almost didn't! George had to propose to me six times before I said yes."

Fred laughed. "Poor guy!"

"I have always viewed marriage as a partnership with dual control. I told him I wouldn't hold him to some medieval code of faithfulness and I was not to be expected to be held to it as well." She lifted her glass and took a drink. "I told him I couldn't guarantee I'd be able to endure the confinement of even an attractive cage!"

Smiling, Fred then questioned. "So, there is hope for me, after all?"

"Time will tell Fred…" Amelia laughed. "Time will tell!"

Back at the airstrip, the scorching sun beat down on the tarmac, creating a shimmering heat haze in the air. In Amelia's absence, they had assigned two local police officers to safeguard her plane. Standing beneath the shadow of the aircraft's wing, they remained stoic and watchful. In the distance, the rumble of engines grew louder as a sleek black car and a modest delivery van approached. The tires of the vehicles screeched to a halt, leaving behind the faint aroma of burning rubber. The driver, clad in a long ebony trench coat, emerged from the car, his confident footsteps echoing on the tarmac. He reached into the depths of his coat and pulled out a large envelope stuffed with a substantial amount of money. A tangible tension accompanied the exchange as he handed it over to the nearest officer. After accepting the envelope, the officer's gaze shifted to his comrade, their eyes briefly meeting. A shared understanding passed between them, concealed behind a subtle smile. In unison, they pivoted on their heels and strode away, leaving the plane unguarded, vulnerable to the world beyond.

••••

The morning sun was rising over two large dunes as Brenda awoke in her tent. With a start, she threw off her blanket without thinking, and instantly stood. Perring down, she searched for any signs of the scorpions she had imagined for the last two mornings.

"You OK?" Jim inquired as he stopped in front of her tent. "Not seeing scorpions, again are you?"

She opened her tent flap and glared. "Go away!"

"Manning has made some great fried spam for breakfast."

Storm's stomach turned. "I think I'll wait for lunch… thanks."

As she turned back inside her tent, he smiled. "Have it your way!"

A few minutes later, she strapped on both of her Colts and walked out into the morning air as Brimmer walked by. "Better hurry! The spam is almost gone!" The light breeze that was blowing through camp shifted and the sharp smell of breakfast filled her nose.

"You all right?" Yadin asked as he passed by.

"I think I just threw up in my mouth.!" she responded softly.

Yadin then laughed. "It's not so bad once you pull all the clear fat off!" At that instant, Storm covered her mouth and ran behind her tent.

"What's with her?" Jim asked Manning.

"I don't think she appreciates my choice of breakfast this morning!"

"Hey Howard… It's your turn to fill our water bladders before we pack up," Jim said as he sat down before the fire. He took the last piece of spam from the small skillet and looked in Storm's direction. "Are you sure you don't want this last piece? Last one loses!"

A minute later, Brimmer walked back into the camp. "We have a major problem!"

"Yeah…" Brenda called out as she drew near. "It's called spam!"

"No, I'm serious!"

"So am I!" she said.

He then took another step forward and shook his head. "All our water is gone!" With the news, everyone's head snapped around to face him.

"What?" came the collective cry of unbelief.

Brenda then questioned. "What are you talking about?"

Brimmer pointed toward the camels. As they neared, Storm's eyes narrowed in disbelief. The sight before her was devastating. Sometime between the previous night's dinner and this morning, an unseen culprit had mercilessly sliced open all the water containers. The air was heavy with desperation as the group gathered around, their expressions mirroring the shock that now filled their hearts. With a sinking feeling, Storm led the way towards the camels. There, hanging from their sides, were the empty containers. No one spoke as they confirmed Brimmers' devastating news. Panic set in, coursing through their veins like a wildfire. Realizing the gravity of the situation, Storm's heart pounded in her chest. In a swift motion, she took four steps backward and reached for her guns, their cold metal weight providing a small sense of security in the face of this dire situation.

"One of you did this!" She screamed.

"Take it easy, Brenda!" Jim called out to calm her hysteria. As he drew near, she pointed the guns in his direction, stopping him dead in his tracks. "Whoa, Brenda… This will not solve our problem here!"

"No?" she cried out. "One of you is trying to stop this expedition… trying to stop me!"

Manning then said. "Maybe it wasn't one of us, maybe it was the Guardians of the Exodus!"

Yadin then said. "Or it could have been desert raiders. They're out here as well!"

"Why?" she asked. "Why would they do this to us?"

Reaching out, Jim shook his head. "This isn't helping, Brenda." He then took a step closer. "We've got to stick together!"

Brimmer then said. "So now what? If we don't have water… we'll all die! No one will get to that plane!"

"Yacasum!" Yadin said softly.

"What?" Jim asked smiling.

Yadin repeated. "Yacasum Oasis! It's an only a half day's ride from here. It's right outside the ruins of Nahal Nappour. There, we will find plenty of water!" Brenda slipped her guns back into their holsters and walked away. Nearing the edge of camp, she stopped and stared into the morning horizon. Jim then approached and stood beside her.

"I don't believe it was the Guardians." Storm announced, as she shook her head and turned to face him.

"Neither do I!"

Storm's eyes grew cold. "It was you!"

"Me?" Jim replied loudly. "Why do you think it was me?"

Brenda folded her arms. "You say you're a photographer but you're not. You carry a .357 Magnum hand gun around with you and you brought along a military shotgun. Not things normal photographers would carry around with them." She shook her head. "You're hiding something, and you sure aren't the person you say you are!" She turned and began walking back to camp. "Whoever you are, Mr. Sutton… or whatever your name really is… I'll find out sooner than later!"

• • • •

Bankok, Siam

June 20, 1937

After completing the pre-flight sequence, Amelia started both Electra engines and slipped on the radio headset. It reported the wind at ten knots coming out of the East and presented no problems for the skilled pilot. Fred sat next to her, making a last-minute check of local airways around them to ensure a safe takeoff, and then gave her the two thumbs-up signal she had come to know so well. Amelia then taxied the plane to the main runway and pushed both throttles forward. As they picked up speed, she felt uneasy.

"Something's not right!" Amelia called over the roar of the engines. They should have been airborne at this speed, but the wheels were still on the turf. She reached out and pushed the throttles again, trying to generate more speed. She then looked at the gauges and said.

"We're above two thousand fifty RPM and still on the ground!" She pulled up harder on the wheel, but nothing changed. Up ahead, she could see the end of the airstrip looming closer with every second. "If I can't get her up soon, we'll end up in those trees!" She pushed the throttle full forward until the engines roared into the red line. The sound within the cabin became deafening as the plane began to rumble and shake. Fifty feet from the end of the runway, the wheels finally left the ground. With a scream of pure adrenaline, Amelia pulled back on the wheel as the tops of the trees brushed the bottom of the fuselage. Once off the ground, things seemed to go back to normal.

"What happened back there?" Fred asked nervously.

Amelia shook her head. "Could have been some crazy down draft from the storm approaching. I'm not sure."

"Is something wrong with the plane?"

Again, she shook her head. "I don't believe so. Everything seems to work now." Rechecking the RPM gauge, she noticed. "Seems like the engines are running hotter than normal, though."

"Should we go back?"

Amelia shook her head for the third time and looked him in the eyes with icy determination.

"Never!" As the plane flew over a small dirt road below them, a man wearing a long black trench coat stood beside his car and looked up with a smile.

• • • •

China Town, San Francisco

June 20, 1937

Greed and domination have always been an underlying factor behind the taming of the Old West and America. Since being founded and given to us as a promised land by the hand of God, it has been corrupted throughout history by individuals only concerned with the wealth it could bring them. It began with the displacement of its early inhabitants, the Native American Indians. Then, in the early 1800s, Chinese nationals came into this country through coercion, kidnapping, bribery, or by their own free will to build the railroad into the multi-million-dollar industry that it would become. The great machine that tied the nation together came at a price few people thought or cared about.

Once completed, the Chinese workers settled together in all the largest cities in the nation. San Francisco, New York, Chicago, and others formed tight-knit communities that left little room or tolerance for outsiders. Within these gathering places, influential leaders sometimes arose and took control, often bringing with them drugs, prostitution, the human slave trade, and gang activities. Local law enforcement was sometimes unable or unwilling to effect any control over the lawless factors.

In 1937, Chinatown in San Francisco was home to the Dragon Cartel. A worldwide organization that delt in the production and distribution of the drug opium. Its organizers supplied hundreds of opium dens in all the major cities in America, each bringing in millions of dollars in revenue for the origination each year. On this night in June, one of the founding members of the Dragon Cartel sat in a yellow DeSoto Skyview taxi cab heading up Grant Avenue toward the very heart of Chinatown. The passenger's name was Sao

Feng. He was young and well dressed in a black pin stripped suit, short cropped black hair, and of Chinese descent. He was born in New York City and brought to San Francisco at a young age by an elderly aunt who hoped for a better life than she had experienced. The life he had chosen to live was not what she had expected.

The dense fog slithered through the deserted street, obscuring visibility to mere yards ahead of the cab. It slinked beneath a web of crimson Chinese lanterns, casting an eerie glow. Amidst the mist, the stench of stale cigarettes invaded Sao Feng's senses, reminding him of his vice. He retrieved a meticulously crafted, solid gold cigarette case from his tailored jacket, opening it with a flick. Placing a cigarette between his lips, he refrained from igniting it. The old, battered cab pulled to the curb when he reached his destination. Sao Feng stepped onto the cracked pavement after hastily handing the driver a crumpled hundred-dollar bill. Walking down the dimly lit, deserted side street, he could hear the distant hum of traffic somewhere in the night. Descending a narrow flight of stairs, he reached a weathered door, its faded paint barely visible in the glow of a solitary, crimson-hued light above. Sao Feng raised his hand and rapped on the door, the sound echoing through the quiet alleyway. The door creaked open, revealing a shadowy figure peering out from the darkness. As soon as they recognized Sao Feng, the figure ushered him inside. Navigating through a labyrinth of closed doors, the figure led him into a room drenched in warm, inviting light. Filled with an exquisite array of artwork, the room held priceless treasures from various corners of the world. He noticed a delicate scent of aged canvas and polished wood, which heightened the room's ambiance. Sao Feng had visited this hidden sanctuary countless times before. The sight of the meticulously curated collection never failed to steal his breath away.

"I hope you have better news!" a voice called out from behind a high-backed chair, laced with frustration. The lingering scent of cigarette smoke wafted through the air, filling the room as Sao Feng approached. The oversized wicker chair, adorned with intricate designs, concealed his business partner, a stunning twenty-eight-year-old natural with flaming red lipstick who called herself 'Tiger Lilly.' As the chair spun around to face him, the sound of its creaking hinges blended with the soft crackle of her burning cigarette. She continued with a hint of impatience, her voice tinged with disappointment. "I hope you have got our money out of Bangkok with no more delays this time!" Sao Feng, his tone defensive, responded,

"I promised you I would, did I not?"

"Well..." she began, her words trailing off as she took a long drag from her cigarette. With a deliberate exhale, she blew the smoke in his direction, the wisps swirling and dissipating in the air. "Your success up to this point had been less than stellar!" Her words hung in the room, filled with frustration and accusation. "You haven't been able to get our money out of that country for three months. That's unacceptable!"

"It's already on its way!" He said.

"Is it?" Tiger Lilly questioned with great skepticism. She flicked the cigarette in his direction, barely missing his head. "How?"

"Are you aware of Amelia Earheart's current flight?" He questioned.

With curt impatience, she replied. "The entire world knows of it! What does she have to do with our money problem?"

Sao Feng took two steps forward and stopped. "Our Bangkok agent hid a million dollars worth of gold bars within her airplane. She will unknowingly fly them to our very doorstep!"

Tiger Lilly's eyes grew narrow. "Won't her plane be searched when it lands?" He said.

"No, she has diplomatic immunity… it's never searched, no matter where she lands. It's a perfect setup for us!"

"Where and when will we be able to retrieve it?" She then inquired. Sao Feng laughed. "Oakland, California… right across the Bay from us!" He then added. "It will be here on the fourth of July."

Lilly nodded. "An Independence Day truly worth celebrating! You've done well!"

• • • •

Sigman Foster sat in an opulent room in the heart of Cairo, the soft glow of candlelight dancing across his face. The rich aroma of the aged liquor filled the air as he savored each sip of his exquisite forty-year-old scotch. A lone piano player skillfully caressed the keys in a secluded corner of the room, filling the space with the enchanting melody of John Lennon's 'Imagine.' He sat within a delicate haze of cigarette smoke, which gently curled above his head, adding a touch of mystique to the atmosphere. After relishing a delectable meal, Foster pushed his empty plate forward, feeling contentment wash over him, and delicately wiped his mouth with the crisp white linen napkin that had graced his lap.

"Care for anything else, sir?" the waiter asked as he refilled Foster's glass.

"No, Jack, that will be fine."

"Excellent, Sir!" He said with a smile. Foster leaned back in his chair and waited as the soft music played. Looking across the room, he watched as Yassin Feisali walked through the crowded dining room and stood at the table.

"Have a seat!" Foster offered. Feisali pulled out the chair across from him and sat down. It was after nine o'clock at night, but the harsh desert still danced upon his brow as large drops of sweat. His hair was unkept, and his sizeable white suit needed pressing.

"You should take more pride in how you look, lad!" Foster then shook his head. "You really are a sight!"

Feisali's brow furrowed. "I'm sure you didn't call me here tonight just to comment on my personal hygiene!"

Foster laughed. "You're right!" He picked up his glass and said. "Have you found pilots for those two flyin' contraptions we confiscated from Burk?"

"You mean the choppers?" Feisali questioned.

"Yes, yes!" He said with annoyance.

"Yes… we've also located a small private plane to fly you to the Saint Catherine Airport." Feisali said. "Our agent on the team tells me

Storm is heading there to meet someone who knows the exact location of Earheart's plane."

"Excellent news!" Foster finished his glass and set it back on the table. "Laddie… here is what I want you to do with those two choppers!"

• • • •

Singapore, Straits Settlements
June 20, 1937

Three hours after leaving Bangkok, Amelia was still fighting to stay ahead of the storm that had plagued their take-off. Five hundred miles into a seven-hundred-and-eighty-mile trip, the Electra ran low on fuel for no apparent reason. It had been a struggle just to get the altitude of three thousand feet, and the engines were running hot.

"I just don't understand it!" Amelia nervously said. "We're experiencing some kind of drag. If I didn't know better, I'd swear it's because we're carrying too much weight!" Fred then offered.

"Maybe something's wrong with the flaps." Amelia turned, straining to see the back of the wings through the cabin windows.

"No... they look fine." As the Storm overtook the plane, it grew dark. With a bright flash of lightning and a crack of thunder, the plane lunged downward. They could hear the loud sound of metal striking metal from behind them.

"What on earth was that?" Fred called out.

"You better go check it out. Maybe one of the extra fuel tanks tore loose!" Amelia said as she checked the gauges. Fred unbuckled and crawled through the small passageway onto the tanks on the other side of the cabin bulkhead. A moment later, he was standing on the other side. From inside the cabin, Amelia called out.

"What do you see?" Fred turned to look at the rear bulkhead that separated the cargo hold from the plane's tail. Just to the right of the door to the toilet, a large access panel had torn loose. Fred's head poked back through the passageway into the cabin a moment later. As Amelia turned to face him, he said.

"You're never going to believe this..."

"What?" she asked nervously. "What did you see?"

"Gold bars... must be at least a thousand of them!" He then smiled as he asked. "Part of the fringe benefits of mass-market product endorsements?"

••••

As Yoko trudged on through the sand, Storm sat upon her back. It was now late afternoon, and the ruins of Napal Napour were sitting in the distance. At one time, Napour was a thriving community of Bedouins who had given up their nomadic lifestyle in favor of a humble existence in the shadow of the palm trees at the Yacasum Oasis. While trading with other local tribes, they had lived a meager life for over a thousand years. Jim rode to Brenda's side as his camel bellowed his disapproval.

"You've been pretty quiet for the last couple of hours… are you all right?"

Brenda looked at the horizon for a moment before she said. "I'm having a problem with one of God's basic principles, and it's bothering me."

Jim's brow furrowed. "Can't imagine you having a problem with anything!" He laughed. "Knowing you, it can't be that bad. Which principal?"

Brenda turned to face him and replied softly. "Forgiveness."

"Who are you struggling to forgive?" Jim asked as their camels moved along.

Brenda turned away again and remained silent as a minute passed before attempting to respond. "The night my family was killed, a young boy named Tim Hargrove played in his last high school football game of the year. After winning, he went to a party with some of his teammates and then attempted to drive the thirty miles to his home." Brenda looked down at the sand passing beneath her and then continued. "It was late, and he got distracted with his cell phone and drifted into our lane." Her eyes then filled with the horrible memory of that night once more. Jim sensed her pain and longed to comfort her as he watched her fight to go on.

"After the trial, the court convicted Tim of vehicular manslaughter and sentenced him to prison. I thought that his prison time would be enough justice for me to feel at peace with what he did. For what he had taken away from me, but it wasn't!" She then shook her head. "I still couldn't forgive him!"

"I'm so sorry!" was the only thing Jim could think of.

After another long silence, she continued. "After being in prison for a little over a year, two other inmates beat him to death over a candy bar." She looked up and wiped her eyes. She laughed. "But you want to know what's really sick? When I heard what happened to him…" As she struggled to continue, a colossal sob found its way into her throat. The following words came rolling forth like an uncontrollable title wave of anguish. "I felt overjoyed!" She then buried her face in her hands and spoke. "I was glad someone had murdered him!"

Not knowing what to say, Jim sat upon his camel and waited as Brenda fought to control her emotions. Without saying another word, she snapped the reins and kicked her camel back into motion. As Jim caught up with her again, she said, "I'm not the wonderful person you thought I was!"

After reaching the oasis, the team repaired and filled the main supply bags with fresh water while preparing and eating a meager meal. Brenda was quiet and kept to herself during most of the evening. She sat alone by the blazing fire long after the others had retired to their tents for the night. Brenda Looked up into the clear night sky and watched as a shooting star streaked overhead. It shocked her when a familiar voice broke the silence.

"Hello, Brenda!" With a start, Storm lowered her head from the stars to see her deceased husband sitting across the fire from her.

"Michael?" She called out in confusion.

"Hey!" He said with a smile. Dressed in the same clothes he wore the night he died; Brenda's brow furrowed.

"Michael?" She repeated a second time.

"Yes, sweety, it's me." He replied with a broad, warm smile. She closed her eyes and shook her head as if trying to shake the image from her view. When she opened them again, he was still there. He laughed and then said. "You can't get rid of me that easy… at least not yet!"

Finally believing what she saw, Brenda's eyes filled with tears as she smiled. "You're really here!"

"Well…" Michael laughed again. "Kinda!" He then grew serious. "But there is a reason for me being here!"

"All that matters to me is that I can see you again!" she said.

"No!" He began. "That's not all that matters!"

"What do you mean?" Brenda asked as she watched the light from the fire dance across his face in the darkness.

"Forgiveness!" The word struck Brenda's heart with such force that it felt like a burning arrow searing her soul. She looked away as if trying to ignore it. "You need to forgive Tim!" Michael pronounced with great sadness.

"How can I forgive him after what he did to you and Rose? After what he did to me?" She shook her head. "How can I ever forgive God for allowing this to happen to our family?"

Michael smiled. "We can choose for ourselves what we do and what we believe. Michael then leaned forward as he continued. "God must let people make mistakes and do bad things to others not because He doesn't care, but because he does! Everyone must have the same freedom to choose; those choices and actions either lead us to Christ or condemn us. There is no middle ground!" Michael smiled again, bringing healing to Brenda's heart.

"Our time upon this earth is but a single heartbeat within the eternal lifespan of our existence. The Lord does not want a moment wasted on anger and hatred toward others and ourselves." Brenda's chest burned as he continued. "Because Rose and I have forgiven him, don't you think you should, too? For it was us, he harmed. The anger toward him you are now holding on to is for your loss, not for ours." With the fire burning between them, Brenda nodded.

"Yes, I can see that!"

"Then, also remember what our brother Jesus Christ has said "He that forgiveth not his brother's trespasses will stand condemned before the Savior, for in him lies the greater sin." As tears rolled down Brenda's face, Michael stood. He turned around and looked into the distance. "There is someone else here that wants to talk to you." Just past him, Brenda saw two figures walking towards them out of the darkness. As they neared the light, she recognized her six-year-old daughter Rose walking hand in hand with Tim Hargrove. When they had reached the fire, all three stood before her.

"Mommy?" Rose said with a smile. "This is my new friend, Timmy!" She looked up into his face and then back to her Moher. "He has something to tell you." Michael, Rose, and Tim all joined hands as Tim spoke.

"I could tell you a million times how sorry I am for what I did, and it would never be enough. I know the pain and heartache I have caused you, and I wish I could go back and change things. To never have made those seemingly unimportant decisions that led to what happened that night." He stood for a moment before going on. "But now... all I can do is seek your forgiveness and pray for the mercy I don't deserve."

Rose then aged before Brenda's eyes into the older spirit that had visited her just after the accident. "Mom..." the adult Rose began as she looked into Brenda's eyes. "The Lord has also said... 'I, the Lord, will forgive whom I will forgive, but of you, it is required to forgive all men!' She smiled. "Tim here deserves your forgiveness. We love him as you should love him, as God loves him!" After wiping her eyes, Brenda nodded with a smile.

"No one is without sin, and only through God can we find relief from the painful burden and find peace from non-forgiveness." A single tear then rolled down Rose's cheek as she added. "Please, Mom... we need you to find the peace you deserve!" With a single sob, Brenda nodded.

"Yes... I forgive you! I'm so sorry that it's taken me so long!" At that moment, a camel bellowed behind her. Brenda spun to face it, and upon returning her gaze to the fire, she saw that the spirits that had once stood before her were now gone. As she sat listening to the crackling fire, she wiped her face from the tears of joy she now shed. She looked up into the clear night sky and watched as a shooting star streaked overhead.

• • • •

The following morning, Brenda found herself alone at the edge of the oasis. Sitting beside the water, she left her gun belt and hiking boots a few feet away. In the distance, Yadin was blasting 'Good Day Sunshine' from his ever-present Beatles MP3 collection. The music felt good for Brenda's soul. Her bare feet were in the water as she played with the moist, cool sand. Beside her, she had made an exact recreation of the ruins of Nahal Napour out of the sand, using her tin cup and small pieces of wood and sticks she had found around the oasis. Deep in thought, she sang along with the music.

"Are you having fun?" Jim asked as he walked up behind her. Startled, she laughed as she turned to see him.

"As a matter of fact, I am!" she said with a smile.

"May I join you?" He then asked.

Brenda nodded. "If you don't think it will hurt your reputation."

Jim sat beside her and momentarily watched as she formed a small wall with the side of her hand. Smiling, he spoke. "I've never seen this side of you before!"

Without looking up, she said. "I have buried it for a long time!" She stopped working and placed her arms on her knees. Looking into his eyes, she said softly. "Hey… I want to apologize for being such a self-centered jerk yesterday! I'm sorry." She smiled and then added. "I hope you can forgive me!"

"Forgiveness?" He responded with wonder. "Seems to be an essential subject in your life." Looking into her eyes, he grew serious. "I need your forgiveness as well."

Brenda's eyes narrowed. "For what?"

"For lying to you!" He replied.

Brenda then laughed. "For telling me you're a photographer?"

Jim shook his head and laughed. "No. I once told you I thought it was a crazy idea that I had feelings for you." He sat silently momentarily, staring into the calm water before him. "Truth is… I've been attracted to you since I first saw you!"

Brenda smiled as she leaned toward him. "Really?"

He then turned and looked into her eyes. "Really!" She placed her hand on his in the sand and drew closer. When their lips were only inches apart, Jim closed his eyes to prepare for a long-awaited kiss.

Brenda then whispered. "I still think it's crazy!" She gleefully tilted her water-filled cup and poured it upon his head at that moment. Jim, taken aback, scrambled to his knees and playfully shoved her, causing her to stumble and splash into the water. Their laughter filled the air as they engaged in a spirited wrestling match, their bodies wriggling like playful children. Amidst the laughter, Jim lifted her and tossed her into the pool's center, a playful act that suddenly turned worrisome when she failed to resurface immediately. Panic surged through him as he called out her name, rushing towards where she had vanished beneath the water's surface. As concern gripped him, she burst forth from below, launching herself at him, propelling them both onto the sandy beach. As they lay intertwined, their gazes locked. Time seemed to freeze, and Jim could feel the warmth of her breath against his face. A whisper escaped his lips, filled with relief. "I thought you were dead!"

Brenda, her lips curving into a mischievous smile, responded. "Would you have missed me?"

"No…" He answered. A moment later, he then added. "That would be crazy!" With their faces only inches apart, something passed between them. Brenda slowly lowered her head and closed her eyes.

"If you guys are finished, we can be on our way," Yadin said with a smile. Looking up, they saw Yadin, Brimmer, and Manning standing above them with folded arms.

"Sorry!" both replied together. As Yadin turned and walked away, he picked 'You've Got to Hide Your Love Away' by the Beatles on his player and pushed play.

••••

As the storm grew around the Electra, Amelia fought to control the bouncing aircraft. With the additional weight of eighteen hundred bars of gold worth over a million dollars, the plane couldn't rise above the turbulence threatening its survival.

"Gold bars?" Amelia called out in confusion. "How did they get on board?"

Fred shook his head from the crawlway. "They had to have been loaded in Bangkok."

Amelia snapped her fingers. "When we were at the hotel!"

"Yeah." Fred agreed. "That's what I figure." At that moment, a bolt of lightning rocked the plane.

"Why would anyone want to hide it on our plane?"

"Is it not obvious? ..." Fred began. "To get it from one place to another without being found."

"Drug money?" She asked as she continued to struggle to keep the plane level.

"That's what I think!" Fred said with a nod. Heavy rain pelted the windshield, creating a roar within the cabin. Looking down at the altitude gauge, Amelia pronounced. "We gotta dump it!"

The unexpected statement hit Fred like a two-by-four.

"What? There's got to be a million dollars in gold back there. Dump it? Are you crazy?"

Her voice growing cold, Amelia answered. "Fred... were going down! There's no place to land, and if we don't lose the weight, we're both going to die!"

"But..." He stammered.

Amelia then turned to face him. "Dump It!" With the ground looming closer, the plane continued to lose altitude. "Hurry!" She called out. "we're down to five hundred feet!"

Fred looked over his shoulder at the pile on the cargo bay floor.

"All of it?" He asked. Amelia's voice grew impatient.

"All of it!"

Looking back into the cabin, he found her eyes and pleaded.

"Every bar?"

As the altitude gauge dropped to four hundred feet, Amelia said. "Every bar!"

Fred shook his head in disappointment and disappeared from the cabin. Making his way to the right fuselage door, he pulled up on the handle and forced it open. As soon as he opened the door, the wind and rain of the storm hit him. Fred moved to the pile of gold and knelt beside it. Picking the first one up, he inspected it.

"Oh, baby…" He spoke. "What you and I could have done together?" Kissing it, he closed his eyes and tossed it out the door. Using both hands and moving as quickly as he could, he emptied the hold of its unexpected and costly cargo. After picking up the very last bar, he hesitated. As if being able to read his mind, Amelia then called out from the cabin.

"Every bar Fred!"

Tossing it toward the door, he said to himself in despair. "I'm really going to regret that!"

• • • •

Soon after leaving the ruins of Nahal Napour, Storm and her group stumbled upon a thirty-mile-long canyon etched into the arid desert floor. The wind howled through the barren expanse, carrying the scent of sand and sunbaked stone. The walls, towering twenty feet high, gleamed under the scorching sun, casting long shadows stretching endlessly.

As the seven camels plodded through the narrow pass, Brimmer's uneasiness grew, intensified by the eerie silence that enveloped the desolate landscape. "This place gives me the creeps!" he muttered, his voice swallowed by the vastness.

Storm chuckled, turning to face him. "That doesn't surprise me. Everything gives you the creeps!"

Looking up at the jagged edges surrounding them, Jim nodded in agreement. "No, he's right!" he said. "This place is straight out of a Twilight Zone episode!"

With a faint smile, Brenda said, "It looks like the place where they filmed Indiana Jones and the Last Crusade."

"That was just a movie. This is real life!" Manning then said.

"This is real life," Jim added as his camel bellowed loudly. "We're headed for the lost plane of Amelia Earhart in the middle of the Sinai desert... I don't know what is if that's not worthy of a Twilight Zone episode."

Brimmer smiled. "Sounds like a great movie to me!" Laughing, he added. "Angelina Jolie could play Brenda!"

Storm's eyebrows furrowed. "Yeah, right!" As they continued to travel along, Brenda moved her camel to Yadin's side.

"So... where are we?"

"This place is called the Nahal Naheeb Canyon." He spoke. Looking up at the massive walls, he continued. "The old ones say that God himself dug it from the desert floor with his finger on his journey to Mount Sinai to meet with Moses. In the wilderness of Sin, the Lord fed manna to Moses and the children of Israel. Exodus chapter sixteen."

Storm smiled. "You know the Bible well!"

Yadin nodded and then said. "This canyon may be the very path of the exodus itself!"

"Wow, that's pretty humbling," Brimmer said softly.

"I don't buy any of it!" Manning added.

Yadin then turned and asked. "You don't believe in God, Mr. Manning?"

"No, not in the least!"

Yadin said with a smile, "Then I'll pray for your soul."

Manning said, "Don't do me any favors, kid!"

"Believe me, the Great Spirit is real!" Yadin said with a conviction that impressed Brenda. She looked in his direction and spoke.

"You and I need to talk."

After a moment of silence, Brimmer said. "I saw a movie once. It was about the crew of a World War Two B-25 bomber plane that crashed in the middle of the desert just like this." He looked up to the sun and shielded his eyes from the glare. "They were all dead, but they didn't know it." He then turned to Manning. "What if that's what happened to us?"

Manning's eyes grew narrow. "What?"

"No, really!" Brimmer exclaimed as he leaned forward. "What if we were all killed by those assassins back in Cairo, and we just don't know it yet?"

Manning laughed. "Wow… you've been out in the sun for too long!" He shook his head and added, "You've gotta stop watching X-Files reruns.!" The group laughed as they continued through the canyon.

Out somewhere in the distance, a low thumping sound echoed through the silence. As the rumbling grew louder, sand and small rocks dislodged themselves from the walls and fell unnoticed to the ground far below. The camels were the first to hear it and stopped dead.

"Listen…" Jim said. "What's that noise?"

"Whatever it is, it's scaring the camels," Yadin replied.

"Forget the camels…" Brimmer began. "It's scaring me!" As the group sat in confusion, the sound continued to grow louder.

Storm then spun on her camel and looked behind them.

"Sounds like…" As she watched, two helicopters appeared within the narrow passage. "Choppers!"

"Maybe Burk showed up to give us a ride!" Brimmer said. The group spun around to see the two choppers approaching them through the narrow canyon.

Shouting, Brimmer began waving franticly. "Hey, We're down here!" Then, suddenly, they heard the unexpected sound of gunfire as bullets started ripping up the surrounding sand.

"I don't think that's Burk!" Jim screamed. Frightened by the sound, the camels bolted away, nearly throwing their riders to the ground.

"Whoa, camel, Whoa!" Brenda yelled as Yoko lunged into a gallop, leaving the others behind. As she disappeared into a cloud of dust, she cried out as she passed the others. "I… hate… camels!"

Burk's two Huey Copters, now being flown by Feisali pilots, continued to advance up the canyon in close pursuit of the caravan. Gunmen sat within each open cargo bay door, raining deadly bullets from American-made military M4 automatic rifles.

"We're all sitting ducks down here! We're never going to make it!" Brimmer yelled out. Racing down the canyon, the camels bellowed in objection.

With the hail of bullets nipping at the camel's heels, Yadin pushed John into a full gallop and took the lead.

"Follow me!" He commanded. "There's a cave up ahead!" Reaching it, the group thundered into the ancient darkness and dismounted. Brimmer dove into the sand and covered his head. As Storm pulled out both of her guns, Jim moved back to his camel and threw open a large rucksack. Moving quickly, he pulled out the shotgun and cocked it with one hand. He then grabbed two large ammunition belts lined with eighty shotgun shells and threw them over his head. After reaching for his holster, he withdrew the large .357 Magnum handgun and spun to face Storm.

"Ready to do this?" He called out with a confident smile. Having just witnessed his movements, Storm stood in shock.

"Just a photographer?" She asked sarcastically.

"Yea!" He said with a laugh. "But I'm a bit busy to take your picture right now!" Smiling, she returned to the cave entrance with Jim close behind.

At the mouth of the cave, they began shooting as the choppers hovering fifteen feet above the ground. Sand, being stirred up by the chopper blades, stung their eyes, making it impossible to hit anything accurately. Soon, the sheer volume of return fire drove them back into the cave.

"Well, this isn't working well!" Brenda said with her back against the wall. As the sound of the choppers outside continued to roar, she turned to look into the cave. As she struggled to see, Yadin walked out of the darkness and stood before them. Below each eye, he had applied two stripes of white paint and carried a bow and arrows over his shoulder. Brenda looked surprised at seeing him and asked. "What are you doing?"

"My father, a full-blooded Cherokee Indian, once taught me about our ancestors who adorned themselves with war paint before stepping into battle," he smiled. "Now, it's time for us to ignite our own battle, to fight for our survival in this treacherous place!"

Brenda's eyes sparkled with excitement as she nodded in agreement. "If we're going to make this official, brother, you better include us in your tribe!" Yadin reached for a container and dipped his thumbs into the thick white substance, his smile growing wider; he streaked the war paint across their cheeks before stepping back, admiring his work.

Jim turned to Brenda, anticipation evident in his voice.

"How do I look?"

Brenda chuckled, her smile contagious.

"Like a pissed-off photographer!" As she turned her attention back to Yadin, she couldn't help but notice the bow in his hands. "What do you intend to do with that against two powerful airborne choppers?"

Yadin retrieved an arrow from his quiver and fit it onto the bowstring. With confidence, he responded,

"I will honor my ancestors and make them proud!" With an understanding of his conviction, Brenda's smile deepened, a shared understanding passing between them.

"There's a tunnel at the end of this cave..." Yadin announced. "it leads up to the top of the bluff. It will put you above the helicopters."

"Good to know!" Storm replied before turning back to Jim.

"Stay here and keep them distracted. I'll go topside and see if I can draw off some of their fire!"

Jim reached out and touched her arm. "Take care of yourself, Brenda Storm. I still haven't taken your picture."

Brenda smiled before vanishing into the darkness. Standing at the cave's mouth, Jim braced himself against the relentless onslaught of the artificial sandstorm, its grains stinging his skin. Looking through the haze, Yadin adjusted his grip on his bow, feeling the string's tension against his fingertips. Bullets whizzed through the air, their sharp cracks echoing through the cave. As he released the arrow, it found its mark, piercing the chest of the nearest gunner. The man let out a scream, tumbling from the chopper to the ground below. Jim's voice boomed in astonishment, barely audible amidst the chaos.

"Nice shot!"

Yadin chuckled, admitting, "Not really... I was aiming for the other guy!"

Jim laughed as he reloaded his weapon with shotgun shells. With a mischievous grin, he turned towards Yadin. "If this were a Die Hard movie, isn't it about time the exhilarating music starts, and Bruce Willis kicks some serious butt?" Yadin's smile mirrored Jim's as he sprinted towards his trusty camel, rummaging through his belongings to find his MP3 player. Selecting a song from his cherished Beatles collection, he pressed play, the familiar chords of 'Help' reverberating through the speakers, adding a touch of whimsy to the battle-scarred landscape.

"That better?" He asked as he returned.

"Much!" Jim said as he fired off the shotgun three times. "Now I can hit something!"

Storm climbed up the rugged tunnel, her hands scraping against its rough stone walls. After emerging onto the cliff's precipice, she felt a warm breeze against her face. Through the rising dust cloud, she saw the two choppers lined up in the canyon before her, their blades whirling close to the unforgiving walls. As the dust settled, she glimpsed the pilots and gunners, their confident smiles visible from her vantage point. They hovered above the cave entrance, awaiting the opportunity to unleash their deadly firepower. Determined to draw their attention, Storm stood tall, planting her feet on the ledge. With both Colts in her hands, she unleashed a hailstorm of bullets towards the lead chopper. The deafening roar of gunfire filled the air. Emptying her clips, she released them, their metal clinking against the rocky ground below. After reloading, she continued her assault, her bullets finding their mark on the chopper's fuselage. In retaliation, the gunner in the first chopper shifted his aim towards Storm.

Knowing what to do, she retreated twenty yards before sprinting towards the edge. At the last possible moment, Storm holstered her guns and lunged headfirst into the air toward the first chopper. With a grunt, she grabbed the right landing strut, her hand tightening around the cold metal. The impact was jarring, the pain radiating through her body. As the chopper veered to the right, the second gunner was violently thrown from the helicopter, falling to his death on the ground below.

The pilot of the second chopper, a wicked grin on his face, saw Storm as an easy target and closed in, his rotor blades menacingly close. Looking down into the pilot's smug face, she could feel the rush of adrenaline coursing through her veins, her heart pounding in her chest. Storm, unwilling to let him succeed, held on for dear life. Her grip tightened as the second chopper inched closer, its deafening roar filling her ears.

Because she needed to free both hands, she pulled her legs up and locked them over the landing strut, allowing her to hang upside down. She felt the wind from the blades only inches from her face as she pulled out her weapons and began firing into the approaching helicopter. One bullet struck the main fuel line and caused the overheated engine to catch fire. While the horrified pilot fought for control, it veered into the high canyon wall and exploded into a ball of flame.

Still hanging upside down, she began firing into the belly of the chopper above her. One of her bullets hit the pilot, sending the Huey into an uncontrolled spin as it descended. At the last second, Storm dropped to the sand just as the tail struck the wall, crashing into the canyon floor. Jim ran through the sand and flames to Brenda's side and touched her unmoving body.

"Brenda? Are you all right?"

Storm slowly turned over and smiled. "Would you have missed me?" Jim then laughed softly. "Yea!"

Yadin stepped behind them and knelt. Laughing, he said with excitement. "Wow... that was Amazing! Who needs a war party when we have Brenda Storm on our side?"

••••

Within the Light

Darwin, Australia
June 28, 1937

Amelia stood upon the right wing of the Electra washing the windows of the plane when Fred emerged from the left fuselage door carrying the fuel supply hose. After filling the six regular and six extra tanks, he had moved back to the two-thousand-gallon tanker truck that sat next to the plane. Replacing the hose, he called out.

"What's next?" Amelia spun to face him as she said.

"The RDF system isn't working. The radio direction finding station here at Darwin said something was wrong. I could hear signals, but couldn't get a bearing."

Fred nodded. "Maybe something happened to it when we almost took out those trees on our takeoff." He thought for a moment and then added. "Might be a fuse in the Bendix coupling unit as well. I'll check it out." Amelia knelt down on the wing as Fred drew closer. "It's imperative that equipment is working. We'll never find Howland Island without it!"

"Gottcha!" He said with a smile. "So… now that our little jaunt is almost over, what are you going to do next?" He then asked.

Amelia sat on the edge of the wing and looked down into Fred's eyes. "Whatever God leads me to!"

"You believe that?" Fred asked with a grimace.

Amelia smiled. "Absolutely!" She reached up and fluffed her hair. "I wouldn't have been able to accomplish what I have without His guidance." Fred's eyes grew narrow. "If there is a God, and I emphasize the word If... don't you think he's got better things to do besides telling you what color crayon to use?"

Amelia laughed. "God is aware of every sparrow that falls from the sky. How much more do you think He cares for you and I?"

Fred then turned away. "God's not done anything for me!"

Amelia's tone grew serious. "God gave His only son, Jesus Christ, to be your savior. His death was for your sins, granting you eternal life. How much more could you ask for?"

He spun around and smiled. "A million dollars in gold bars?"

Amelia shook her head. "You couldn't have taken it with you if we would have died!"

Looking up, Fred replied. "Yea, I suppose you have a point," he admitted. Smiling, he then added. "But it sure would have been fun to try!"

• • • •

At the base of Mount Sinai, Saint Catherine has been a working monastery since its creation in the fourth century. According to Christian beliefs, they executed a saint named Dorothea in AD 294 for converting to Christianity. Angels placed her body on the mountain top and then disappeared. Three centuries later, monks guided by a dream found it and placed it within a golden casket. They then placed it within the monastery, which would later become known as Saint Catherine. It became a gathering place of world religions and a sanctuary for those seeking God.

Outside its stone walls, Sigman Foster stood talking to Yassin Feisali.

"Well, Laddie... what good news do you bring me of Storm's death?" Foster inquired with a grin of expectation as he wiped the sweat from his brow.

"Not good!" Feisali said. Then, expecting the worst, he took a step back. "Storm and her group destroyed both helicopters... there were no survivors!"

"What?" Foster screamed. "That's impossible!" He took two steps forward and grabbed Feisali's robes. "How could a wee lass, two college geeks and a child, defeat eight trained assassins and bring down two military choppers?" Foster then added. "How is that even possible?" Pushing him to the ground, Foster turned away. "How much time before they reach this place?"

Feisali climbed back to his feet. "Two, maybe three days."

Foster turned to face him again. "Then we have little time to find that guide!"

By late afternoon, Storm had grown tired of riding, feeling the ache in her muscles as she now led Yoko along behind her as her team continued their journey southward. The looming mountain range and a series of low cliffs created a sense of isolation and grandeur. Yadin, as usual, had taken the lead. He had swapped his usual happy-go-lucky attitude for a more somber mood, reflected in the choice of music he was playing through the speakers. The melancholic melody of a Beatles song floated through the air, evoking a sense of nostalgia and sadness. Today was April tenth, the anniversary of the Beatles breakup in 1970. As they moved across the valley, the familiar strains of 'Let It Be' resonated across the shallow valley. Amidst this backdrop, Jim walked up beside Brenda, a warm smile illuminating his face.

"Hey!"

"Hey!" she said without diverting her gaze from the bright horizon. Walking in silence for a moment, Jim then looked at her.

"How are you holding up?"

She turned to him and said. "Fine, thank you." For the first time in his life, Jim was feeling nervous around the opposite sex. With Brenda, he felt out of his league. Not feeling sure how to proceed with the relationship, or even if there was a relationship at all. He was walking in unexplored territory, and it was blatantly obvious.

"So… what caused your change of heart last night?" Jim inquired as he pulled on Paul's reins.

Brenda smiled, but didn't look at him. "Forgiveness."

"Ahh…" Jim said. "There's that magical word again."

She then turned to him and found his uncovered eye. "You know... it really is magical now that you mention it." She then continued. "It can take the deepest pain and resentment away."

Jim then said. "Well, I'm glad you feel that way because I have something else to tell you!"

After Laughing, Brenda replied. "You mean besides what you told me this morning?"

Looking away in embarrassment, Jim chuckled. "Yea." He then turned to her. "I've been needing to tell you for a while. And now after this morning... I really need to tell you."

Brenda's smile vanished as confusion took its place. "Wait... something's different about you today!"

Jim looked down at himself as his brow furrowed. "What? What are you talking about?"

After Staring closer, Brenda shook her head. "No, something has changed about you!"

Jim laughed. "I'm just the same as I've always been."

Then suddenly, she realized what it was. "Your eye patch..." she said. "it's on the wrong eye!"

Jim immediately reached up and moved the patch back to the other eye. "Ummm..." He lied. "My eye doctor told me to use my bad eye now and again to strengthen it!" Not believing him, Brenda stopped dead in her tracks. Manning and Brimmer then caught up with them.

"Who are you?" she demanded as she dropped Yoko's reins.

Brimmer then called out. "What's going on?",

Spinning to face him, Brenda yelled. "Shut up!" Then, turning back, she ripped the eye patch from his head. She pulled out her gun and asked again. "Tell me who you are!"

"I was just about to!" Jim replied in frustration. He took a step toward her and explained. "My real name is not Sutton... Its Walsh. Garrett Walsh!"

"So, what else is new?" Brenda spat out.

"And I'm not a photographer!"

Storm folded her arms. "No kidding!"

Taking another step closer, he added. "I'm a field agent from the CIA. I'm here to protect you and this project."

"Protect me?" she exclaimed; her voice filled with fury. With a swift movement, she pulled back her arm and unleashed a powerful right cross, connecting with a satisfying thud against Walsh's chin. The impact sent him hurtling backward, his body soaring through the air before crashing onto the sand five feet away. As Walsh lay sprawled on his back, Brenda stood over him, a mischievous smile playing on her lips. She approached him, kneeling down by his side as he struggled to sit up. The faint scent of desert sand filled the air as Brenda's fiery eyes bore into Walsh's. "Does that look like I need your protection?" she taunted; her voice laced with satisfaction. Her hand jabbed forward, her finger pointing at his face as she unleashed her anger. "That's for lying to me!" she shouted. With a swift movement, Brenda reached out and grabbed Walsh's shirt through the opening in his robes, pulling his face inches away from hers. The heat of the desert sun beat down on them, intensifying the charged atmosphere. "And this..." she declared, her voice softer now, "Is because I forgive you." Brenda then pulled Walsh those last two inches closer and pressed her lips against his, their passionate kiss a testament to their tumultuous relationship. But before they could indulge in the moment, Yadin's voice cut through the air.

"I hate to be the one who keeps breaking you two lovebirds apart..." Yadin's words drifted towards them as he approached on his camel. Brenda and Walsh broke apart, their faces flushed with a mix of desire and frustration. Yadin's gaze shifted to the nearby cliffs, his eyes scanning the landscape. From both sides of the cliffs, the sound of approaching hoofbeats filled the air, growing louder with each passing second. Thirty mounted riders, dressed in vibrant robes, came into view. In the desert sunlight, the colors seemed to vibrate with energy, enhancing the scene with a touch of magnificence. As Walsh and Storm rose to their feet, Brimmer's voice broke the silence, barely audible above the commotion.

"Guardians of the Exodus?"

Yadin shook his head. "No. Not this time in afraid. They're Bedouin desert raiders!"

Inside his robes, Walsh placed his hand on his gun. "Are they friendly?"

"Not usually!" Yadin replied. Brenda then withdrew her guns. Looking down at her, Yadin shook his head again. "Put those away or we're all dead!" The two groups stood in silence, looking at each other until Manning spoke.

"So... what do we do now?"

Yadin brought his camel to its knees and dismounted. "Wait and see what they want."

"What if they want to kill us?" Brimmer stuttered.

"Well..." Yadin said. "If that's the case, it was nice knowing you." Three riders descended the small slope and made their way to face them. As they drew near, their rifles and swords glistened in the sun. The remaining raiders waited on the ridges with their rifles in hand.

"I am Sheik Emir Abdullah Aviv." The center raider announced. "Who are you and why have you come to my desert?"

Walsh moved forward and spoke. "Your desert?"

Giving him a stern look, Yadin then faced Aviv. "A million pardons Sheik Aviv. We only travel though your desert on a pilgrimage to Saint Catherin. We seek nothing more than your permission to do so."

Aviv looked at the loaded pack camels and pointed. "If that is true, why do you carry so many supplies?" Storm grew nervous, and looking at Walsh, something passed between them.

"We come from a great distance and need supplies to survive." Yadin replied. The Sheik dismounted from his black stallion and walked to face Brenda. He pulled the white wrap from around her head to expose her face. As Walsh lunged forward, the remaining riders leveled their rifles upon him.

Aviv looked at Yadin and asked. "Who is this infidel woman?" Aviv's voice boomed, filled with contempt.

Brenda, taken aback, furrowed her brow and crossed her arms. "Excuse me?" she retorted. "My name is Brenda Sto..." Before she could finish her introduction, Aviv's hand struck across her face, the sound of the slap echoing through the air. Brenda's left hand instinctively shot out, grabbing onto Aviv's flowing robes, her fingers tightening in their grip. With her right hand, she pressed the cold metal of her gun under his neck; the touch sending a shiver down Aviv's spine. "You hit me again, Sheikie," she warned, her voice laced with a dangerous calmness, "and I'll paint this sand with your brains. Do you understand?" In the blink of an eye, the remaining raiders galloped down, surrounding the small group of travelers. With rifles raised, the raiders filled the tense atmosphere with metallic clicks. Brenda maintained her grip on Aviv, her gun still pressed against his skin. Her voice, barely above a whisper, carried a deadly promise. "I suggest you tell your friends to back off, or they'll be needing a new leader." After a moment of silence, the Sheik smiled and turned to face the raiders. Speaking in Arabic, his words brought them raucous laughter. Brenda's brow furrowed; her annoyance clear. She then pushed the gun harder into his chin. "That wasn't a nice thing to say about me," she remarked, her tone tinged with annoyance. Aviv's surprise flickered in his eyes. "You speak Arabic?" he asked incredulously.

Brenda's smile revealed a hint of pride. "I speak six languages... it's all part of my job," she said.

Aviv called out to one of his horsemen, who dismounted and approached Brenda, a rifle aimed at her head. Aviv's voice dripped with menace. "Now," he began, "you can put your gun down and live, or your entire group will meet their end. The choice is yours." A smirk played across his face. "I'm not afraid of death... are you?" Brenda locked eyes with Walsh, who then nodded. After a moment, she reluctantly released her grip and handed her gun over to Aviv.

"You have great spirit. So much so I have never seen in a woman." After speaking again in Arabic, they also met it with laughter. "You will do well!"

"With what?" Brenda questioned.

"As my sixteenth wife!" He said with a laugh.

"No!" Walsh cried out. The dismounted raider struck him with his rifle butt, bringing him to his knees.

"I'll never marry you!" Brenda screamed. With another nod from Aviv, the raider placed his rifle to Walsh's head.

"Come with me or I'll kill them all!"

"Go!" Walsh called out. "We'll find a way out of this, I promise!"

• • • •

Within the expansive tent of Sheik Aviv, the warm glow of dozens of flickering candles illuminated the encroaching darkness of the desert. The air was heavy with the scent of roasted chicken, mingled with the faint aroma of burning incense. The tent itself stood as a sanctuary amidst the harsh nomadic existence of the Bedouins, adorned with opulent treasures accumulated over generations of oil production in the Middle East. Exquisite rugs, meticulously crafted pillows, and beautiful blankets adorned the space, creating an ambiance of prosperity and worldly indulgence. Two imposing guards ushered Brenda into the tent, her hands bound by heavy chains. Then, they forcefully brought her to her knees before the Sheik, who reclined upon a lavish pile of cushions. The Sheik, savoring the moment, gently placed a grape in his mouth. With a mixture of admiration and amusement, he addressed Brenda. "If you had not overcome four of my strongest guards, I wouldn't have had to place you in irons, my dear Miss Storm. It's really not worthy of such beauty as yours."

Brenda couldn't help but laugh, her voice ringing out amidst the richness of the surroundings.

"Maybe you should think about getting stronger guards!"

Placing another grape in his mouth, he replied with a laugh. "Maybe so." He then leaned forward and inquired. "Do you know who I am?" Brenda smiled again. "You're an over inflated, egotistical troglodyte with a severe case of brain envy!"

Aviv laughed again. "You have a fiery spirit I truly admire!"

Standing back up in defiance, she replied. "Well... don't get used to it, bub... I don't plan on being here very long!" With a smile, he gestured with his hands.

"Please, please... have a seat!" He then added. "Make yourself comfortable."

Holding her hands out in front of her, she stated with a smirk. "That's kind of hard to do with these on!"

Aviv leaned back again and asked. "If I have them removed, will you promise not to overpower my guards again?"

After a moment of silence, she said. "Maybe..."

"Ahhh... that's what I like about you. Pure honesty in a relationship."

"Don't get any ideas, Sparky." Brenda began, "This is not a relationship!" Aviv looked at the waiting guards at her side and nodded. After unlocking her chains, both left the tent, leaving Brenda and Aviv alone.

"You are a very brave woman, Miss Storm."

"I'm desperate!" Brenda began. "And desperation breeds bravery."

"Or foolishness." The Sheik added. "I'm a wealthy man and there's not much I don't get if I want it." Brenda moved to the pillows in front of him and sat down. She reached out and took a grape from the solid gold bowl. With a smile, she looked into his cold, dark eyes.

"I got a fortune cookie once that said he who takes what is not his to take wakes up with a knife in his back!"

Aviv smiled. "That's very interesting, but I have never found that to be a problem."

Popping another grape into her mouth, Brenda smiled. "Well... not yet!"

Aviv stood and began walking toward an enormous banquet table loaded with food. "I am... the head of the Saint Catherine's Research Center at the University of the Arts in London, England. We raise awareness of the monastery's cultural significance through lectures, books, fund raisers and articles in the most prestigious publications in the world." Brenda's brow furrowed. "Are you trying to impress me?" Picking up a two-hundred-year-old wine bottle, he began pouring it into two of his finest imported crystal goblets.

"Your young friend said you were going there to worship. Maybe we have more in common than you suspect!" returning to her side, he offered Brenda the glass. "Care for some wine?"

With a smile, she waved it off. "No, thank you. I don't indulge in anything that affects my reflexes."

"Ahhh." Aviv reacted with a smile. "I admire that." Placing her glass down, he added. "I also gave up drinking when I was at Princeton. It interfered with my studies."

Brenda grew interested. "When were you at Princeton?"

"I left two years ago."

With a smile of wonder, Brenda confided. "So did I!"

Aviv grew excited. He put his glass down and leaned closer. "What was your field of study?"

Brenda laughed. "I hold a doctorate in anthropology and antiquities!" Aviv nodded. "This is simply amazing!"

"What were you there for?" Brenda asked.

"Geological Engineering and Business Administration. I've lived most of my life in America."

"Really?" Brenda smiled. "I never would have expected that."

"Please..." Aviv began. "I haven't lived with goats my whole life!" Thinking a moment, the excitement of their shared experience passed, and Brenda returned to reality.

"You must have also excelled in Chauvinistics 101." She said as she pulled away from him.

He then looked at her in embarrassment. "Sorry... I might have been just a bit out of line when we first met. I have a reputation to uphold in front of my tribe. Please believe I'm truly sorry!"

"A bit?" Brenda shot back with cold indignation. "You can't expect me to marry you!"

Aviv picked up his glass and emptied it before responding. "I have a lot to offer you!"

Brenda looked into his eyes and spoke. "Sorry... the answer is still no!" Aviv clapped his hands twice and four of the Sheik's Bedouin wives entered the tent and stood waiting at the entrance, dressed in beautiful silks of many colors.

"I must insist you consider my offer for a bit longer, Miss Storm." He then gestured to the women. "My wives will prepare you for our Zuara Celebration to be held tomorrow night." He smiled. "There, we will ask Allah to bless our tribe with abundance and fertile wombs!"

"Whoa!" Brenda said. "That's not a blessing I need right now!" The wives then moved to her as she stood. Again, commanding something in Arabic, Aviv watched as they then led Brenda from his tent and into the waiting darkness.

· · · ·

Lae, New Guinea

July 2, 1937 2:45 am

After flying twenty-two thousand miles around the equator, Earheart and Noonan took off from Lae, New Guinea, with only three stops remaining of their round-the-world flight. After Leaving Lae, their next refueling stop was a tiny, two-mile-long, less-than-a-mile-wide dot called Howland Island in the Pacific Ocean. The Electra's Ventral antenna on the underside of the fuselage had become damaged and unusable without being noticed during their last take-off on the turf runway.

The United States Coast Guard cutter Itasca, anchored off the shore of Howland, had received orders to assist Earheart in locating the island by using two-way radio communications and transmitting signals for a directional location. They would soon find all of these useless without the undiscovered damaged antenna's help.

"So… if you don't believe in God, what do you think happens when we die?" Amelia asked as she readjusted the pilot's seat.

While scanning a chart, Fred replied without looking up. "Haven't given it much thought."

Amelia smiled. "Well… now's a good time to think about it!" In frustration, he placed the map on his lap and exhaled.

"I don't know Amelia… I guess we become worm food!"

She then turned her head to face him. "And that's it?"

"Yea!" He said as he refocused on his job.

"You don't believe that, do you?"

Fred's temper grew short. His following few words came out slow and deliberate. "Yes… I do!"

"Then how do you explain it?" She responded.

Fred turned to face her in exasperation. "Explain what, Amelia?"

She laughed and pointed out into the darkness. "The whole universe!... me, you... Life?"

Shaking his head, Fred replied in aggravation. "You know this is useless, right?"

"Maybe." She said with a grin. "I'm just trying to save your soul!"

"Look…" He laughed. "I appreciate your concern, but why don't you just focus on saving my sanity by getting us back to Oakland? Sitting in this plane has left me utterly drained."

As she slipped on her radio headset, Amelia tuned the radio to 3105 KHZ and spoke. "This is Earheart KHAQQ to Coast Guard cutter Itasca. Do you read? Over." With no reply, she reached down and double-checked the broadcast setting. Finding it correctly, she tried again. "This is Earheart KHAQQ calling Itasca. Do you read? Over." Fred looked up and saw Amelia's concerned eyes. "This is KHAQQ. We are at one thousand feet on target for Howland Island. Weather conditions are cloudy. We have limited visibility. Over." In her headset, she could hear only the sound of static.

On board the Itasca, radio operator Leo Bellarts sat in the radio control room as Amelia's calls came in. He responded and acknowledged her call but received no reply to verify she had received it. He then grew concerned and contacted the Captain and told him about the grave situation the flight was now facing.

• • • •

After leaving Brimmer and Manning behind, Yadin and Walsh had followed Aviv's trail for over four exhausting hours before the fading daylight forced them to halt. Yadin settled beside a crackling fire, its warm glow casting dancing shadows on his weary face. Returning from his camel, Walsh retrieved the shotgun from its worn leather holster and joined Yadin by the fire. The soft melody of "Let It Be" by the Beatles filled the air, carried by the portable sound system—Yadin's gaze fixed upon the sinking sun, its vibrant hues blending with the horizon. A heavy sigh escaped his lips, carrying a tinge of sadness.

"The worst event ever to occur in human history!"

Walsh laughed. "Um... was it the invention of platform shoes?"

Yadin's brow furrowed. "No! The breakup of the Beatles in 1970." Going back to loading, Walsh smiled. "If you say so, kid."

"And it was all Yoko's fault!" Yadin added in disgust.

Walsh stopped and looked confused as he spoke. "Wow... and I always believed that the walrus did it!" Yadin turned with a cold, dirty gaze, knowing that Walsh had meant his comment to upset him. After a minute of silence, he questioned.

"We're outnumbered. What's the plan once we catch up to them?" When Walsh finished loading, he twirled the gun to his shoulder and looked down its sight.

"How brave are you?"

Yadin smiled. "As brave as I need to be."

Walsh Lowered his gun and spoke. "When we find their camp, we'll wait for the cover of darkness and then make our move. We should be able to get in and out before they know we are there!"

Yadin said. "I'll have the Warpaint ready if we need it. But for now, we better get some sleep." He threw a few more small sticks into the fire and lay down. "We'll need to get an early start to catch them!"

• • • •

Within Sheik Aviv's tent the following night, the tribe's leaders had gathered for the Eid-al-Adha, the feast of sacrifice. Part of the Zuara Celebration was a time for retrospect and appeals to Allah for prosperity and health in the future. Also in attendance were the tribe's religious leader, Aviv's wives, and a handful of armed guards. Brenda sat in the white silks of prospective wives next to Aviv, at the head of the group. A costume she had fought hard and long to avoid.

"My fellow countrymen, we are here to celebrate Allah's mercy and love toward each of us tonight," Aviv said as he stood. Dressed in his finest silk and satin robes, his charm and charisma were beyond most of the men Brenda had ever met. She could now see how he had risen to the power and authority he had achieved. She looked around at the many faces before her and realized the devotion and love they had for their leader. His position within the world had allowed him to do much for his tribe and the welfare of the Bedouin people in his country. For all his faults as a person, Brenda could now see him as the caring, self-sacrificing person he was.

Brenda smiled despite herself as the sweet smell of sandalwood incense floated through the candle-lit tent and mixed with roasted chicken and cinnamon aroma. As Aviv continued to speak, her heart softened, and she admired her captor for what he was trying to accomplish. Outside in the darkness, gunfire echoed across the desert as a guard ran into the tent.

"We are being attacked, Your Highness!" As he gasped for breath, the guard added.

"A group of riders from the South!"

As the others turned to face the panicked guard, Aviv called out. "Who is it?" Hesitating for only a moment, the guard replied.

"It's your brother… Aaron!"

"Gather the warriors!" Aviv's commanding voice reverberated through the air. The sound of his words hung heavy amidst the chaos. Men scrambled to their feet, their hurried footsteps creating a symphony of thuds and rustling. Aviv's gaze settled on one of his remaining guards as the commotion grew. With a firm voice, he instructed, "Take my wives to safety and protect them with your life!" His face etched with loyalty, the guard drew his sword and nodded in unwavering obedience. He swiftly turned towards the entrance; his every movement filled with purpose. But before the guard could take another step, a sudden eruption shattered the tense atmosphere. A bullet, fired from outside, tore through the air with a piercing sound, finding its target in the guard. The impact brought him down, his body collapsing in a heap of bravery and sacrifice. Brenda then leaped to her feet.

"What's going on?" She questioned as she turned to face Aviv.

"My brother has long opposed my position within our family. He has now grown bolder and intends to usurp my power by killing me!" Brenda swiftly turned, her senses heightened, just in time to witness a guard stumbling into the tent, a dagger protruding from his back. He took another step and fell to the floor. Aviv seized a sword in a desperate bid to protect his loved ones, his movements a blur of determination. The metallic clash of blades reverberated as he fought fiercely against one of his brother's men. Every strike and parry sent tremors of adrenaline coursing through Aviv's veins, his heart pounding in his chest.

"Get my wives to safety!" He screamed as he glanced at Brenda. "Please!" As Brenda moved, the raging battle outside grew louder. Screams and gunshots rang in her ears as she gathered the surrounding women. She froze as a man riding a great black stallion entered the tent. His horse was richly adorned with silver and gold, and a hood of red satin covered its head. As it galloped in, its finely braided mane and tail filled with precious stones flew as if on the wings of a mighty angelic bird. The rider pulled a rifle from the saddle and pointed it at Aviv.

"Stop!" He called out. The fighting ceased, and, noticing Brenda's movement, the man on foot grabbed her from behind and held her arms. The wives began screaming and cowered at her feet.

"Nice to see you again, my brother!" Aviv spoke as he dropped his sword to the ground. "It's too bad it has to be under such unfortunate circumstances!"

Aaron Kept his rifle leveled on him and replied. "I'm taking back what is mine, brother! Father should have left our family wealth to me. I am the eldest son!"

Aviv's brow furrowed. "You were in line to receive everything but went against our father's wishes! You forced him to make the decision that he did!"

Angry, Aaron leaned forward in the saddle. "More of your lies!"

"You brought shame to our family; you followed the priests of Sin. To follow in their evil ways and forsake Allah. It was you who have caused this, not I!"

"Shut up!" Aaron screamed.

Aviv took a step forward and continued. "You are the one who sacrificed our only sister to your God!" He screamed back. "It was you!"

Aaron then replied with an evil, unearthly smile. "And now, my dear brother, you shall die as well." As the weight of the rifle settled against his shoulder, the metallic click of the trigger echoed through the tent. Her heart racing, Brenda leaned forward, her muscles coiling like a spring. With all the power she could muster, she jerked her head backward. With a sickening crack, her skull connected with the man's nose as it broke. Pain pierced the man's face, and he doubled over, a guttural scream escaping his lips. Brenda wasted no time, her body moving with fluid grace. She spun on her heels, her knee striking precisely, forcing him to his knees. With a final blow, her powerful right cross sent him crashing into unconsciousness. Aaron sat frozen, his eyes wide with shock, unable to comprehend the whirlwind of events unfolding before him. Brenda spun and, at a full run, tackled him from his horse, the thud of impact vibrating through their bodies. Standing with his sword in hand, Aviv loomed over his defenseless brother. His cold steel caught the candlelight, casting a deadly gleam. Brenda's instincts kicked in as he raised the sword above his head, ready to deliver a fatal blow. Without hesitation, she positioned herself between the two brothers as a shield of protection.

"Don't do this!" she said.

Fighting to control his great anger, Aviv replied. "He has soiled our family name!"

Storm reached up and placed her hand on his. With a smile, she said. "He has soiled his name, not yours. Allah would have you take mercy upon him."

Breathing heavily, Aviv lowered the sword. "You're right, Brenda Storm! Thank you." He then tossed the sword to the side and turned to walk away. At that moment, Aaron grabbed Aviv's sword and standing, raised it to strike his brother in the back. Before delivering the death blow, a gunshot rang out within the tent. Aviv and Storm spun just in time to see Aaron fall to his death. Confused, they saw one of Aviv's wives holding a smoking rifle.

"Someone's coming this way!" Yadin called out to Walsh as they walked toward Aviv's camp. The moon was full and lit the surrounding desert. They had sat within its glow and waited as the sound of gunfire drifted through the night air. Now that it had grown quiet again, they continued to creep toward their destination.

"Did you miss me?" A voice called out from the darkness.

"Storm?" Walsh cried in confusion. "Is that you?" As they watched, Brenda came riding out of the dark on a black stallion adorned with silver and gold.

"What are you doing here?" She asked with a smile as she drew closer and stopped.

"Well…" Walsh laughed. "we came to rescue you from the Sheik." Brenda prodded the horse back into a trot and said, as she passed them.

"Oh, that was nice… thank you!"

• • • •

Howland Island

July 2, 1937   7:40 am

Tension was running high within the Electra as Amelia and Noonan continued to search for Howland Island. With the rising sun it hampered visual location by the scattered clouds that now dotted the ocean below them. Shadows from the clouds fell upon the water, making it difficult to distinguish any land masses they would have been able to detect. After completing a navigational sun line estimate, Fred figured they should be within fifty miles of the island. After looking down at the fuel gauge, Amelia spoke.

"We're almost out of fuel, Fred. If we can't find that island soon…"

"I know!" Fred whispered. "I know!"

Amelia then asked. "Can you see anything down there?"

Fred strained to see out the side cockpit window. "Too many clouds." He then turned to face her. "Try the radio again!"

"They can't hear us, and I'm not getting any RDF signals from the ship."

"Please…" Fred asked. "Just keep trying."

"KHAQQ calling Itasca. We must be on you, but we can't see you. We are online North and South at 157 337. Over." As in all previous attempts, the only response came as light static in Amelia's ears. "What do you think is wrong, Fred?" She pleaded with misty eyes.

"Something's got to be wrong with the ventral antenna. I've checked out the Bendix receiver, and it's working fine." He shook his head. "We're just not able to receive anything."

"Do you think they're hearing us?"

Fred nodded. "Probably."

Amelia then flicked the fuel gauge, hoping it would change. When it didn't, she shook her head. "Well, Fred… we need a miracle. Are you ready to believe in God yet?"

Laughing, Fred replied. "The only miracle we could receive at this point would be to find that island."

Closing her eyes, she said. "Then I'll pray for the both of us."

••••

The township of Wadi el Deir surrounds the walled monastery of Saint Catherine. It has several schools, a hospital, police and fire brigades, and various hotels and restaurants. Because of its location, the monastery and surrounding areas are of great worldwide religious importance to Jews, Muslims, and Christians, and it receives more than one hundred thousand visitors a year. Each comes to witness for themselves and receive a personal testimony of the things spoken of in the Bible. Storm and her team were preparing for the new day in one of the better hotels.

After walking from the bathroom, Garrett Walsh carried a white bath towel to dry his hair after his cool shower.

"That's better!" Manning said as he sat in the corner reading an English newspaper. "You still smell like a camel, but at least it's bearable now!" Yadin laughed as he finished tying his black high-top tennis shoes. Brimmer sat oblivious to everything else as he watched the Brady Bunch on the room's big screen TV.

After throwing down his towel, Walsh asked, "Where's Brenda?"

Yadin then answered, "Our contact isn't meeting with us for a couple of hours, so she went shopping."

"Shopping?" Walsh repeated with furrowed brows. "Alone?"

Yadin laughed. "That's what she said."

Finding his gun, Walsh threw on a shirt and walked out into the sunshine. The township was bustling with tourists walking through the shop-filled streets as Walsh began his search. Along with the many tourists, seven thousand Bedouin citizens from six tribes comprised the rest of the local population. As he hurried along a narrow street, it impressed him with its somewhat modern look within the shadow of such an ancient structure.

Looking into a clothes boutique, Walsh found her. She smiled as he drew near.

"Here to protect me?" Walsh stood at her side and smiled as she pulled a fine-knitted shawl from the shelf and tossed it over her shoulder. Then, turning to a mirror, she found her reflection.

"Kind of hard to hide two Colts under something like that, wouldn't you say?" Walsh asked with a soft laugh.

After she replaced it, she said. "Yeah, I guess so." With a tinge of sadness, she added. "It's not very practical in my field."

"But it looked good on you!"

She touched it again and asked. "You really think so?"

"Befitting a sheik's wife!" Walsh kidded with a smile. Storm turned and threw a dirty look in his direction before returning to the busy street. "It's funny…" Walsh said.

"What?"

He looked around and gestured with his hand to the crowd. "I can't believe that with all the people in this place, no one else has found Earheart's plane!"

As they continued to walk, Brenda spoke. "Maybe God only wants us to know about it."

Walsh's brow furrowed. "Why?"

Tossing a street vendor, a coin, she picked out a pear and took a bite without stopping. "Haven't you ever heard that God works in mysterious ways?"

"Maybe." He spoke.

"Nothing is chance in this world. God arranges things if it benefits his children." She explained as she continued to scan each shop as they walked by.

Walsh then said, "So, you think He arranged for you and me to meet?"

Brenda turned and found his eyes. "Maybe."

"Remind me later to thank Him!" He said with a grin.

She then stopped and turned to face him and asked. "Do you believe in God, Mr. Walsh?"

He looked deeply into her eyes. "I'm still collecting evidence."

She then began walking again. "Don't waste time you can never get back. It's too precious."

"I'll remember that." He said as he moved to her side. "Why is this place so popular?"

"This is where it all started." She said with a smile.

"Where what started?"

"The Exodus!" Brenda answered. She stopped, examined a beautiful dyed goat-skin bag hanging from a rack, and then turned to face him. "Many things written in the Bible occurred in or around Saint Catherine. The rock of Moses, now called Hagar Musa, is in Wadi el Arbain. It's believed to be the rock from which Moses brought water to sustain the Children of Israel." Walsh nodded as Brenda continued. "Within the monastery itself lies Saint Helen's chapel, where a living bush believed to be the same one Moses saw burning but not consumed as he spoke with God."

"I take it you've been here before?" Walsh questioned as they moved again.

She spoke. "Twice in the last two years. Once for work, and once on vacation."

He laughed and then said. "I'll stick with Disneyland!"

Brenda broke into an enormous grin as excitement filled her eyes. "You don't feel the spirit of God on the Dumbo ride!" She spoke. She then exclaimed. "I live for this stuff! It's why I went into Anthropology!"

Looking at his watch, Walsh then replied. "We better be returning soon, or Yadin will leave us behind!"

Brenda laughed and then grabbed his hand. "I want to visit only one more place before we head back. It will only take a few minutes!" Storm pulled him along, heading down a deserted side street. Soon, they were walking into a beautiful walled garden against the mountainside. Brenda led Walsh up a narrow path to one of her favorite spots in the city. On one side of the dirt trail was a bench, and on the other was a large flat rock supported by three larger stones.

"What is this place?" Walsh questioned as he looked around.

"It's called the 'wishing rock,'" Brenda said. "According to local legend, if you throw a pebble and it stays on the top, your wish will come true."

"Oh, Really?" He replied as his eyebrow lifted in curiosity. She pushed him down onto the stone bench and sat beside him. She then picked up a small rock and closed her eyes. After a moment, she smiled and gently tossed the tiny stone. Bouncing twice, it came to rest on the top. She turned to Walsh and smiled.

"Now, it's your turn!"

"Are you going to tell me what you wished for?" He asked as he picked up a pebble.

"Nope!" Was Brenda's reply.

"Fine!" He said as he closed his eyes and smiled. After seconds passed, he giggled to himself.

"This is serious!" Brenda called out, laughing.

"Sorry!" Walsh offered. He closed his eyes again and concentrated. He opened them a few seconds later and tossed the small rock. It skipped across the top and also came to rest on the edge.

When Brenda looked back to face him, he kissed her deeply. "Wow…" she whispered as he pulled away.

"That's what I wished for!" Walsh announced.

As Brenda moved to kiss him back, she smiled. "Me too!"

• • • •

As Brenda and Walsh returned to the business district, people haggling over prices filled the air. Large groups of tourists led around by overpaid, nasal-voiced women carrying clipboards wandered aimlessly through the streets, searching for the following insignificant location. As they walked to a pottery shop, Brenda approached an outside table and picked up a large, brightly painted clay vase. She then held it up for Walsh to see and inquired.

"What do you think of this one?" Brenda asked, her voice filled with excitement. The bustling street was alive with car horns and people chattering. Suddenly, a deafening gunshot echoed through the air, causing panic to erupt. The delicate vase in Brenda's hand shattered into a million pieces, a cascade of shards glinting in the sunlight.

"Get down!" Walsh screamed; his voice drowned out by the surrounding panic. He acted, pushing Brenda to the ground as a bowl on a nearby table exploded into fragments. Both of them instinctively reached for their guns, their faces etched with confusion. Amidst the onslaught of bullets, Brenda called out,

"Did you see where it's coming from?" The air was dense with gunfire, the sound seeming to come from all directions.

Walsh replied, his voice laced with a hint of dark humor, "No... but I hope you didn't have your heart set on that vase!" He glanced over the table cluttered with broken pottery, his eyes scanning for an escape route. "Although, you could probably get it for pretty cheap about now!" Taking hold of Brenda's hand, he wasted no time pulling her towards an open door leading into the pottery shop. The moment they stepped inside, the overpowering smell of clay and dust surrounded them. Undeterred, they forged ahead, their determined footsteps drowned out by the terrifying symphony of bullets narrowly missing them.

As they reached the back door, Brenda's brow furrowed with concern. "You think Feisali's behind this?" she questioned; her voice tinged with unease.

Walsh responded, "Who else would want us dead in the middle of this desert?" With a firm grip on Brenda's hand, he swung open the door, revealing a foul-smelling alley. At the crossroads of the alley, Walsh scanned their surroundings, his senses heightened by the imminent danger. Just as Feisali's men emerged from the shop behind them, Walsh and Brenda sprinted towards two young Bedouin men sitting on motorcycles a short distance away. In a split second, Walsh stood upright, his hand reaching for his wallet. With a swift motion, he flipped it open, revealing his New York City library card. With a poker face, he delivered his line with utmost seriousness.

"My name is Jean-Luk Picard from the World Transportation Organization. I have found your motorcycle unsafe for public use! I have to take it back to our office and impound it!" Instantly, the young man got off and backed away. Walsh climbed on and, holding down the clutch, kickstarted the bike. With Brenda behind him, they vanished down the busy street. Only moments later, without a word, one of Feisali's men shoved the second rider from his bike and took his place. As the second gunman jumped on the back, both riders roared off in close pursuit. As they gained speed, Walsh began weaving through the tourists and locals, who continued to walk through the crowded streets, oblivious to what was happening around them.

Feisali's men began shooting as they drew closer. Walsh's heart stopped cold as he watched three camels being led across the street in their path. Not having time to change direction, he then cried out to Storm.

"Low bridge!" All three camels lined up at the last second, allowing the motorcycle to go beneath them at forty-five miles per hour. As it skidded to a stop, the second bike had to wait for the camels to pass. On the opposite side of the camels, a large wooden cart stood tilted, obstructing the middle of the bustling street. With thunderous acceleration, Walsh soared onto the improvised ramp and launched into the air, then landed on the roof of a vibrant yellow and red tour bus. Inside, the tour guide's eyes widened as she witnessed the unfolding spectacle, attempting to maintain composure among the bewildered passengers.

"You are all in for a rare treat today. If you gaze out the windows, you'll witness our tour bus being utilized to film an electrifying James Bond action-adventure movie!" Her words sparked a frenzy of excitement among the twenty-two passengers who clamored to capture the extraordinary scene with their cameras. Meanwhile, the motorcycle carrying Feisali's two men circled the cart, aiming their weapons at Brenda and Walsh, who maneuvered their cycle across the bus's rooftop. At that moment, two stray bullets pierced through the back window, shattering the glass and cascading onto the startled tourists.

A teenage boy then exclaimed, "Wow... those special effects look so real!" Just moments later, after an adrenaline-fueled sprint along the bus's length, the motorcycle leaped off the front, landing on the roof of a nearby car, triggering a blaring alarm. Undeterred, Walsh pressed on, hurtling down the street at full speed.

Storm then yelled into Walsh's ear. "Wow, that was fun, but what will you do for an encore?"

He shook his head and spoke. "Don't know, but I'll try to figure something out!" Still racing down the street, both cycles grew closer as bullets continued to fly. Brenda pulled out one of her guns and, half turning, began shooting back while Walsh gained speed in his attempt to escape. In the turmoil's heart, dozens of frightened pedestrians sought refuge, clear of the thundering danger now heading for them. Just ahead of Walsh, two carts stopped side by side, blocking the street.

"Hold on!" He screamed as he skidded in a new direction.

Abish Niebuhr was a sixty-two-year-old Bedouin woman and mother of two children. She had lived a hard life, and her body had become frail from years of hard work in the blazing summer heat and the cold Sinai winters. She was a religious woman of great faith and served hundreds within her community. Before her husband died, he had been the garden caretaker at the Monastery of Cosmas and Damianos. Now alone, she was facing a significant decision in her long life. Her son and daughter wanted her to travel back to Cairo to be with them. She had been fasting and praying for three days but, as yet, had not received an answer.

On this day, she had made her way to the chapel of Saint John Klimakos seeking guidance. They built the large stone structure in 1979 to commemorate John Climacuss's devotional work in the sixth century. His book, ' The Ladder of Divine Ascent,' was a guide to attaining spiritual glory with God. Abish walked down the center aisle between the wooden benches before a large twenty-foot-high stained-glass window behind a raised pulpit at the front of the room. Halfway into the chapel, she moved down one bench on the right side. She found a spot that felt right and sat down. She then closed her eyes and knelt in supplication.

"Allah... please send me a sign that I may know if I should travel to join my two children," Abish whispered, her voice filled with desperation and hope. Walsh, his eyes fixed on the open doors of Saint Klimakos chapel, revved the motorcycle's engine, feeling a surge of adrenaline coursing through his veins. The twelve stone steps leading up to the chapel seemed to blur as he shifted into a higher gear, the engine roaring in response to his command. Bracing himself, he yelled to Storm, his voice swallowed by the wind.

"Hang on!" The motorcycle propelled forward with a burst of power, defying gravity soaring through the front doors. As they landed halfway down the center of the aisle, the sound reverberated off the ancient walls, echoing through the air. Abish, her eyes snapping open, witnessed the spectacle unfolding before her, a divine sign urging her to swiftly journey to her beloved son and daughter. She looked towards the heavens, tears streaming down her face, and whispered,

"Praise be to Allah!" Without hesitation, Walsh and Brenda soared up the four steps to the pulpit stage, the motorcycle again defying the laws of gravity. The momentary weightlessness filled their bodies with exhilaration, their hearts pounding. The crashing sound of shattering glass followed them as they burst through the vibrant stained-glass window, shards glittering like diamonds. As they landed back on the street, Walsh gripped the brakes, bringing the motorcycle to a skidding halt, the tires leaving behind black streaks on the pavement. Brenda, her laughter bubbling up, slid off the back of the bike, her heart filled with a newfound sense of adventure.

"You really know how to show a girl a good time!" she exclaimed; her voice filled with excitement.

"What are you doing? Get back on!" Walsh called out in confusion. "They'll be here any second!"

"Go!" Brenda yelled. "I'll catch up with you!"

"Don't do anything stupid!" Walsh's urgent voice echoed through the narrow alleyway. As his sleek cycle roared away, Brenda maneuvered between the towering buildings, seeking refuge in the veil of shadows. Moments later, the pursuing motorcycle careened around the chapel's weathered wall, racing past her with thunderous speed. Emerging from her concealed location, Storm's heart raced as she retrieved her twin guns, their presence comforting in her hands. With focused determination, she aimed. Satisfaction coursed through her veins as one of her last bullets found its mark, piercing the rear tire. She holstered her guns, a triumphant smile gracing her lips as she witnessed the once powerful cycle lose control, its tires skidding and fishtailing wildly. The moment's chaos led the out-of-control motorcycle to crash into a low stone wall, propelling both riders over the handlebars and into a repugnant mound of dung and decaying straw. Brenda's brows knitted together in contemplation, her mind searching for a distant memory as she muttered,

"Now... where have I seen that before?"

• • • •

Howland Island

July 2, 1937 8:45 am

Inside the Itasca radio room, Commander Richard E. Black, in control of the Howland Island airstrip, stood with the Captain and radio man Leo Bellarts.

"So, what seems to be the problem, son?" Commander Black asked as he drew near.

"The signal strength of Earheart's last three messages shows she's close, sir… in the immediate area."

"So, what's the problem, then?" He questioned.

"Sir… the RDF equipment aboard this ship won't work above 550 kHz. Earheart is transmitting at 3105 kHz. Because they aren't receiving voice communications, I can't tell them to switch to our wavelength!" Bellarts looked up into Black's eyes and said. "I'm sitting here sweating blood because I can't do a darn thing about it!"

Black then turned to the Captain. "Use your oil-fired boilers to generate a dark column of smoke. They might see it over the horizon!"

"Great idea, Richard!" The Captain said. "Meanwhile, see if you can send a message using Morse Code. It may be our last hope!"

Amelia opened her eyes inside the Electra and reached for the radio control. "This is Earheart KHAQQ. We are on line 157 337. We will repeat this message. We will repeat this on 6210 Kilocycles…"

Fred shook his head. "Wait."

Amelia took off her headphones and turned to face him. A look of confusion then filled her eyes as she spoke. "What?"

"You're wasting your time. There's no sign they're receiving us. Save your breath."

Amelia looked into his eyes. "It's not like you to give up, Fred!"

"Face it, Amelia..." He spoke. "This is the end of the line! At that moment, the dots and dashes of the Morse Code message began coming in.

Surprised, Amelia questioned. "You wouldn't know Morse Code, would you?"

Sadly, Fred then replied. "No, and it's a bit too late to learn it now." Thinking a moment, he turned to her. "Can you use it to gain a bearing?"

Amelia worked at the RDF receiver and then said. "I can't get a lock on it." She Slipped her headphones back on and broadcasted her last message. "This is KHAQQ." She Looked up at her compass and reported. "We are running online North and South. I received the Morse Code but was unable to determine their direction. Over." The mood then changed within the cockpit. With all hope now gone, the only thing left was acceptance that they would never see another day. Never get the chance to live a full life. With this acceptance came a quiet peace that fell upon them like a soft summer rain.

"Well..." Fred then said. "I guess it's now OK to tell you... I'm in love with you."

"Really?" Amelia joked. "I hadn't noticed." She reached over and touched his arm. "It's been an honor knowing you, Fred, I..." At that second, the plane rocked.

"Is that the end of our gas?" Fred inquired.

Amelia looked down at the fuel gauge and shook her head. "No, not totally!"

"Then what was that?" He questioned.

She checked the gauges and looked at the engines. "I'm not sure." Out ahead of the plane, a strange cloud began forming. Its swirling mass rotated counterclockwise ways and grew more prominent by the second. Within its center, a light radiated with an unusual brightness.

Upon seeing it, Fred pointed as he exclaimed. "What on earth is that?"

Amelia's brow furrowed. "I've never seen a storm cloud do that before."

Fred shook his head. "That's no storm cloud!"

"Then what is it?" Amelia questioned. Nothing had ever frightened her until now in all her years of flying, and nothing she had ever seen looked this unearthly. Moments passed as the light in the center grew brighter.

When the plane grew closer, Fred warned. "Since I'm your navigator, I strongly suggest we not fly into that thing. Whatever it is!"

Nodding, Amelia gripped the wheel. "I'll have to agree with you on this one, Fred!" As she attempted to change direction, she found the wheel and rudder frozen. "I can't change direction!" She called out. Without being able to look away from the light, she added. "It seems to be pulling us in."

"What?" Fred questioned.

"Nothing is working… I can't keep us from going into the light!" Within seconds, the blinding light filled the cockpit and enveloped Amelia and Fred in a calming warmth that seemed to penetrate their very souls. Amelia felt at peace, and her mind flashed images of her life. Playing out like a movie, she watched herself experiencing precious memories that made her smile. She saw her family at Christmas time and the happy hours she had spent with her younger sister, Grace. She witnessed her first flight and subsequent trips into the sky that would define who she would later become. Once the memories had faded to white, it was over. Within the light and total silence that followed it, Amelia closed her eyes and left the world questioning her fate for over seventy-five years.

• • • •

The Electra

Within the boarding stable nestled near the hotel, Walsh stood beside Paul, his camel. As he carefully packed his belongings into the rucksack, he could hear the faint rustling of straw. The earthy scent of the stable engulfed the room. Stepping back, He gazed into Paul's eyes, a warm smile gracing his lips. Tenderly, he rubbed the camel's neck, feeling the coarse texture of its fur against his fingertips.

"You're a good boy, Paul. I've always liked you best," he murmured. In response, the camel turned its head towards him, contentedly chewing on a mouthful of straw. It blew air from its nostrils, a gesture of his appreciation. A sudden noise jolted Walsh out of his reverie. Instinctively, he reached for his gun, eyes scanning the dimly lit stable. He slowly headed for the unknown sound, and with each step he took across the dirt floor, a soft crunch reverberated beneath his boots. As Walsh drew closer, a small hole in the roof allowed a sliver of light to pierce through, casting a spotlight-like beam through the dusty air. The particles danced gracefully as if choreographed by an unseen hand. A thought crossed Walsh's mind, and he chuckled softly, imagining that Yadin, given the choice, would have chosen a Beatles song as the soundtrack to this ethereal display. Finally reaching an isolated stall, Walsh's breath caught in his throat. There, amidst the straw, Brenda knelt in prayer, bathed in the angelic beam of light. The sight was nothing short of breathtaking. He slowly holstered his gun, standing in awe of the scene before him. Images of the baby Jesus in a manger flooded his mind, evoking memories of Christmas. Although he had not grown up with religion, he was now confronted with an inexplicable and incredible experience. Walsh silently absorbed the moment, allowing the spirit radiating from Brenda's countenance to envelop him. He knelt beside her, his heart filled with awe and embarrassment. Gently, she opened her eyes and whispered, her voice barely audible.

"Sorry… I didn't know anyone else was in here."

Walsh then said. "Don't apologize, it was beautiful!"

Brenda's brow furrowed. "Was I praying out loud?"

Laughing, he replied. "Oh no, not that. Just you sitting here in this light." Brenda looked upwards and smiled as the beam warmed her face. "My father used to call those 'fingers of God'".

"Well…" He began. "It was a beautiful sight to behold."

"Thank you." She spoke.

"What's it like?"

"What's what like?"

"Praying." He replied.

Brenda's head pulled back in surprise. "You've never prayed?"

Walsh shook his head. "No, never! But I've always wondered why people do it?"

Brenda thought for a moment. "Are your parents still alive?"

Looking up into the light, he nodded. "My Mother is."

"Do you call her?"

With a quick nod, Walsh replied. "Sure, sometimes."

Brenda then asked. "Does she love you and want to know how you are doing?"

"Sure…" he began. "Doesn't every parent?"

Brenda reached out and touched his arm. "Well, you have a heavenly father who loves you and wants you to succeed. Praying is how we talk to each other."

Walsh smiled. "Oh, I get it!" His brow then furrowed. "Is that why you said you don't believe in chance?"

Laughing, she said. "Yep… God's hand is always in our lives whether we recognize it or not."

"So, what were you praying for just now?" Walsh asked.

Biting her lip, Brenda thought for a moment. "Safety, success… forgiveness."

Walsh laughed. "Ahh, there's that word again."

"Oh…," she began with a smile. "I also thanked Him for not letting you kill us this morning!"

Walsh nodded. "Yeah, for sure." He picked up a small stalk of straw and looked at it. "God seems to be a big part of everything!"

She nodded her head in agreement.

Walsh then looked deeply into her eyes. "I wish I was as sure of things as you are." With a furrowed brow, he asked, "How do you know for sure that God is real? That He's there?"

"It starts with the tiny seed of wanting to know… wanting to believe. It starts with recognizing the Holy Spirit." She then asked, "Tell me… you said when you saw me praying that it was beautiful. Why did you say that?"

Walsh sat in silence for a moment. "I don't know. I felt this warmth. Something that gave me goosebumps. Something that made me feel emotional."

Brenda nodded as she smiled. "That feeling was the Holy Ghost. It sometimes testifies to heavenly truth." She then added, "It's all part of the gospel." As Brenda spoke, the light above her highlighted the edges of her hair and rested in her eyes, causing them to twinkle with life.

"There's something within your eyes that I don't see in most people." He spoke.

"When I'm not punching out camels?" She laughed.

"Brenda, I'm serious!" Walsh scolded.

"Sorry. I'm just not used to this kind of conversation. I have so many faults that I don't see myself that way most of the time." She turned to face him. "I just do the best I can most of the time." She then stood and asked. "Do you want to know why I'm the way I am?"

"Please…" He replied. "I do!"

Brenda then spun, returned to the camels, and rummaged through her rucksack until she found what she had been searching for. Returning to her spot in the light, she sat down and handed him her Bible.

"I want you to have this."

"What is it?" Walsh asked as he took it from her hands.

"It's my instruction manual for life!" She answered as she brushed a loose strand of hair from her face.

As he opened it, he found a handwritten inscription from Brenda's father. He looked up into Brenda's eyes.

"Go ahead, read it!" She requested.

He then began reading it out loud.

> *My dearest daughter,*
> *On this, your eighth birthday, I give to you my most valued possession. Within this book, you will come to know and love God our Heavenly Father. There is nothing of greater worth that I could give you at this special time in your life. May you find it as comforting and helpful in your times of need or the happiest moments as I have.*
> *I love you dearly.*
>
> *Your father.*

He looked up with moist eyes, turned to her, and handed it back.

"Brenda, I can't keep this!"

Wiping her eyes with the back of her hand, she pushed it back toward him. "Then just give it back when you're done reading it!" An impressive silence fell upon them momentarily as the holy spirit filled the room. It was a feeling of peace that touched their very souls. Walsh stared at the book, rubbed his hand across its cover, and nodded. Brenda then reached out and touched his arm.

"Read it, and then ask God with a sincere heart if it's true or not. The Holy Ghost is powerful, and you've taken the first step in recognizing it and have felt it within your heart." Walsh then rose to his feet and held out his hand to Brenda. When she took it, she stood and said. "Read the book, Garrett. The spirit of God is what you see in my eyes. It's as simple as that."

As they stood face to face, Yadin called out as he entered the stable. "Hey guys… do I have to separate you two again?" Walsh and

Storm smiled and began walking toward him as Manning entered with a middle-aged Bedouin woman following close behind.

"This is Sofora Yigael. She's going to be our guide to the plane." Yadin said as Storm grew close.

"Hello!" Walsh said as he offered his hand.

Brenda nodded once. "Thank you for helping us."

Brimmer walked in as Yadin approached one of the pack camels.

"I hope I'm not too late for the party!"

Yadin opened a large bag hanging from his shoulder and began pulling out sticks of red dynamite and shoving them into a large sack upon the animal.

"Where on earth did you find those?" Walsh laughed.

Yadin smiled. "Let's just say someone owed me a favor."

"Why do we even need those?" Brimmer asked.

"I figure with all the problems with Feisali, Aviv, and the Guardians of the Exodus, we could use as much firepower as we could get!"

Walsh then nodded. "Sounds good to me!"

"All right, kids!" Storm shouted while she mounted her camel. "Let's all go solve a seventy-five-year-old mystery!" As the group moved out into the bright afternoon sunlight, 'Magical Mystery Tour' by the Beatles began playing in the background.

• • • •

Their guide became agitated as the caravan wound around Mount Sinai's base. Sofora Yigael, like most Bedouins, was religious and feared the power of Allah. She looked at the top of the mountain with deep trepidation as something happened. Within minutes, the surrounding air filled with significant plumes of dark smoke and flames as they drew closer. The earth shook beneath them, bringing an uneasy feeling to those who now rode below the turmoil.

As the rumbling grew louder, Yadin quoted loudly as he looked up. "And mount Sinai was altogether on smoke because the Lord descended upon it in fire and the smoke thereof ascended as the smoke of a furnace, and the whole mount quaked. Thunders and lightnings, thick clouds upon the mount." He looked at Brenda and smiled. "Exodus chapter nineteen, verse eighteen." Just then, lightning struck the mountaintop, followed by heavy thunder.

"This place is giving me the creeps!" Brimmer exclaimed, his voice filled with unease. They had been trekking through a narrow passage for an eternity, the dim light casting eerie shadows on the surrounding walls. Finally, after covering another four miles, they arrived at a small canyon with towering walls. It felt like they had stumbled upon a forgotten realm frozen in time. Amelia's airplane sat in the canyon's center, a ghostly monument from a bygone era. It stood there, alone and haunting, its presence a reminder of the most famous missing person mystery that had baffled the world for over seventy-five years. Goosebumps prickled Storm's skin. Her breath caught in her throat. A deafening crack split the air as they cautiously moved forward, and a lightning bolt seared the ground just inches ahead of Yadin's camel. The animal let out a terrified bellow, sending shivers down their spines. Yigael shouted in Arabic, her voice panicked, and swiftly turned her camel around. She rode back alone, leaving the rest of them stunned. In the tense silence that followed, Walsh spoke up, his voice quivering with curiosity. "What did she say?"

As she looked up at the smoking mountaintop, Brenda replied. "She said that this place is sacred and we should leave here. That God was angry, we are desecrating a holy place."

Brimmer then whistled the Twilight Zone theme song.

"Maybe we should do what she says!" Manning pronounced.

"No!" Brenda replied with determination. "We've come too far to give up now!" On the cliff above them, two riders from the Guardians of the Exodus sat watching them.

Walsh was the first to see them. "Well…they haven't tried to stop us yet." He noted. Brenda and the others sat silently and watched them for any sign of reaction. Walsh pulled the shotgun from its place.

"Let's not provoke them if we can help it," Storm said as she looked into Walsh's eyes.

As he slipped it back, he nodded. "Got it."

Keeping her eyes on the riders, she then prodded Yoko onward. Once reaching the plane, they pulled the camels to a halt and sat in awe at what stood before them. At an early age, Brenda adopted Amelia Earheart as a role model and idolized her accomplishments and exploits as an example of what women could accomplish. Besides all the reading she had done about her life and disappearance, she also had made several trips to the Smithsonian to view her Lockheed Vega 5B, which she had purchased in 1930. In this small plane she called her 'Little Bus,' she flew nonstop and alone across the Atlantic Ocean, which made her the first woman and only person since Charles Lindbergh to do it. Now, seeing this plane she had disappeared in almost eighty years ago made her respect for the Vega pale in comparison. To the group's amazement, the aircraft looked like someone had just constructed it yesterday. The dazzling aluminum body and twin tail shimmered under the blazing Sinai sun, emitting a radiant glow that defied its age. The plane gave the impression of being frozen in time in this spot, with no evidence of the passing years. Brenda dismounted her camel, her feet sinking into the warm sand, and approached the aircraft. She gently pressed her hand against its sun-warmed fuselage, relishing the smoothness beneath her fingertips. Closing her eyes, a content smile spread across her face, overwhelmed by a sense of fulfillment.

"Don't get your hopes up, Storm!" Manning's voice called out. "We still lack concrete evidence that this is Earheart's plane!"

Turning her gaze towards him, she stood her ground. "It is... I can sense it!"

As Walsh joined them, he looked at the plane and then spoke. "So... what's the plan to tackle this project?"

After lowering her hand from the side of the plane, Brenda turned to face him. "Let's set up camp first before we get too involved." She pointed to a spot to the left of the plane and continued. "We'll set up the operations tent there and the others behind it." Yadin nodded and began leading the pack animals to her suggested location. Within two hours, they had set the camp up. The operations tent, measuring twenty feet by twelve, contained forensic lab equipment, blueprints, schematics of the Electra, and all the written information on the flight and disappearance. In one corner, they set up a table and medical tools needed for autopsy, isolating them with thick plastic sheeting.

With Walsh by her side, Storm secured the satellite internet connection to three silver laptop computers lined up before her and pulled a handful of files from a brown leather pouch. She placed them on the folding table and stood. Walsh followed her outside, and she hooked up the solar-powered generator to the central power line.

Walsh smiled. "I was told you were the best at what you do. Now I can see why."

Brenda laughed. "I don't know about that, but I've never followed the path and chose instead to go where there is no path and leave a trail for others to follow."

"Well…" Walsh began. "I would consider this a different path!" As he looked at the plane, he added. "I'm just thankful I could be a part of this!"

"Even after I punched you out?"

Walsh laughed. "Yeah… even then!" Once the camp was in order, the group focused on why they were there. Carrying a clipboard, Brenda walked beneath the left wing and looked up.

"What's that?" Yadin inquired as he followed her gaze to a set of numbers and letters painted on the underside of the wing above them.

"In July 1936, Purdue University paid for a custom-built Lockheed Electra 10E for Amelia Earheart. They made it at Lockheed's Burbank California plant, and its registration number was NR16020." Brenda said. She then pointed upward and smiled. "Same as that!"

"Proves nothing!" Manning sternly denounced as he walked up.

Growing frustrated, Brenda spun to face him. "You've been finding every occasion you can to cast doubt on this project!" She folded her arms and asked. "What's it going to take to convince you?"

Shaking his head, Manning replied. "Not just some painted numbers on a wing and someone stupid enough to fall for it!" With his remark, Brenda balled up her fists and began walking toward him, only to be stopped at the last minute by Walsh.

He then turned to face Manning. "Might be a good idea for you to go count some bolts or something until she calms down a bit!" After watching him leave, Walsh turned back to face her.

"What? Me calm down?" she replied with a laugh. "And stop being Brenda Storm?" She then shook her head. "Never happen!"

"Both fuselage doors are locked!" Yadin called out as he came around the plane. "I can't get in that way." His brow then furrowed. "But I think I can see a body through the cabin window."

"Right side or left?" Storm asked as she moved out in front of the plane to look for herself.

"Right," Yadin answered.

"Climb on the wing and see if you can get a closer look," Brenda suggested. Moving around to the back, he jumped to the wing and went up to the windows.

"I can't see inside very well. The windows are murky." He said as he spun from the glass. Just then, an earthquake shook the plane, causing Yadin to lose his balance. Being shaken from his place within the navigator's seat, Fred Noonan's body slumped sideways, causing his head to slam against the side window just as Yadin drew closer for another look. Noonan's empty eyes, staring coldly at nothing, shook Yadin to the core. With a scream, he pulled away from the window, fell backward onto the wing, and rolled off into the sand.

"What happened?" Storm yelled as she knelt by his side.

"Someone's in there!" He said in deep fear. "And it's not someone who's been dead for seventy-five years!"

"What?" Walsh cried out as he joined Brenda at Yadin's side. "What do you mean?"

"If that guy up there is dead... he's not been dead very long! I've seen plenty of corpses left in the desert a long time..." He then pointed to the cockpit and continued with a shaken voice. "And that guy is not one of them!" Looking up, Walsh then stood and headed for the main supply tent.

"Where are you going?" Brenda questioned as she watched him walk away.

"To find something to break open that door!"

"No!" she cried as she stood. "This plane has survived for seventy-five years. We can't be the ones to destroy it now!" She spun and looked at the cabin.

"There's another way in!"

Walsh stopped and spun to face her. "Where?"

As she walked back to the front of the plane with the others following, Brenda looked up. "There's an access panel above the pilot's seat on the left side. All we have to do is remove a few bolts."

Looking at Yadin, Walsh said. "Go get the toolbox out of the tent!" Yadin stood and, shaking his head, pointed upward. "I'm not going anywhere near the dead guy!"

Manning then walked forward and spoke. "He's right! This place is cursed. We should all leave here now!"

Brenda spun to face him and angrily pointed. "You say one more word, and I swear, I'll shoot you right here and now!" After retrieving the toolbox, Walsh climbed to the cockpit with Brenda close behind. After removing eight bolts, he pulled the thin aluminum access panel from the fuselage.

Brimmer then said. "Being the forensic expert, I should be the one to go in first."

Walsh pulled out his gun and climbed to the roof, slipping his legs into the open hatchway. "I'm going in first. We don't know what to expect in there."

Brimmer nodded. "OK, but touch nothing!" Walsh nodded and then disappeared into the cabin. As soon as he had lowered himself into the empty pilot's seat, Walsh felt something he had never felt before. As he saw the inside of the plane for the first time, he felt a strange calmness that rested upon him like a warm blanket on a cold winter's night. He felt as though he had traveled back in time as he looked at the black and white rudimentary gauges before him.

Looking to his right, he then focused on the body beside him. He had been in close contact with dead bodies before, but this time, seeing Noonan, he didn't feel the usual uneasiness he had felt so many times before. He could detect no signs of injury, and if he hadn't known better, he could have sworn he was only sleeping with his head against the window.

When presented with a dead body, the first thing Walsh always did was check for a pulse. Upon doing that, he quickly pulled his hand back in surprise. There was no heartbeat or pulse, but his body was as warm as if he were still alive. He pulled Noonan's body back to sitting and looked into his face. His eyes stayed open, but strangely, he couldn't detect any signs of decomposition or rigor mortis in the body. He climbed through the crawlspace and over the extra fuel tanks behind the cabin bulkhead and moved across the cargo bay to unlock the fuselage door. As he did so, he noticed that his watch had stopped and showed the incorrect 8:49 am. Opening the door, he jumped down into the sand below. As Storm and Brimmer approached, he lifted his wrist to reset his watch but found it running again at the correct time. Not thinking much of it, he shook his head.

"Last time I buy a cheap knockoff watch online!" He announced to himself in disgust.

Nearing him, Brenda then asked. "What was that all about?"

Walsh laughed as he turned to face her. "Oh... nothing important!"

• • • •

Standing at the open door, Brenda looked in. "Where is Earheart's body?"

Walsh shook his head. "I don't know, but It's not in there!"

Her head then snapped around. "Then where is it?"

Laughing, he replied. "How would I know?"

Stepping up into the plane, Storm's confusion grew as she said. "It's got to be in there someplace!"

"Trust me, it's not!" After entering the plane, Brimmer followed Brenda into the cargo hold with a small forensic case. He climbed into the cabin and then sat in the pilot's seat, where he opened the case. Then, for the first time, he looked into Noonan's face.

"What's going on here? Is this some sort of sick joke?" He asked in confusion as he looked back through the cabin crawl space.

As he peered through the opening, Brenda's brow furrowed. "What's the problem?"

Brimmer reached over and touched Noonan's face with the palm of his hand. Shaking his head, he said. "Whoever this is, he's not been dead for seventy-five years!" He took out a laser thermometer from the case and held it above the dead man's forehead. After a moment, it read 97.6 degrees. "That's impossible!" He whispered to himself in unbelief.

Brenda then grew closer. "What's impossible?" Before replying, he took another reading and got the same results.

"A normal healthy body temperature is 98.6 degrees. Once dead, the temperature drops one degree every hour until the body reaches room temperature."

"OK…" Brenda began. "So, what's so impossible?"

Bremmer grew silent for a moment and then said. "This body's temperature is 97.6 degrees, which means this guy has only been dead less than an hour!"

"That's impossible!" Brenda said.

Brimmer then smiled. "That's what I just said!"

"There must be something wrong with your equipment," Brenda said. He then shook his head. "No… I checked it twice!" Brimmer reached out and lifted the body's arm and let it drop back to its original resting place on his lap. He then poked Noonan's face with his fingertip. Looking back to Brenda, he pronounced. "There's no sign of rigor mortis or decomposition... at all. Both are indications of the correct time of death. I'll know more once I perform a full autopsy." He spoke. "Walsh! Get the stretcher. We need to take the body to the tent." Upon his return, they placed the stretcher on the cargo bay floor and removed the body from the cabin. Placing it on the stretcher, Bremmer opened his case again and pulled out a small voice recorder.

"What's that for?" Walsh inquired.

"I keep a full recorded record of what I find and what I've done for future reference."

Walsh nodded. "I see".

Turning it on, Brimmer spoke into it. "Alleged body of Fred Noonan found aboard a Lockheed 10E in the Sinai Peninsula. The exact time now is…" He Looked down at his watch and frowned. Turning to Brenda, he then asked. "My watch seems to have stopped. What time is it?"

"That's strange…" she said as she checked her watch. "Mine has stopped as well."

With a distant voice, Walsh drew near them. "They wouldn't both be reading 8:49 am, would they?"

Both of their heads snapped up to look into Walsh's eyes. "Yes… how did you know that?"

He held out his watch and spoke. "Because mine says the same thing!" He stood in confusion and then said. "And what's weird is that this is the second time today that it happened to me, and both times it stopped at 8:49 am."

Brenda turned to Brimmer. "What do you think would cause that?"

"I don't know!" Smiling, he then added. "Looks like we have more than one mystery to solve here." Replacing his recorder, Brimmer pronounced. "Until we find out what's going on here, I suggest we keep the body onboard the plane for now!"

As the evening campfire burned, the shadow of its flame danced upon the canyon walls around them. Its eerie glow contrasts heavily with the jet-black sky filled with a million points of heavenly light overhead. With dinner eaten, Brenda sat with Walsh before the blaze as Brimmer approached.

"Well…" he began. "I got a DNA sample from the body and compared it to the sample of a living Noonan relative."

"And?" Brenda asked with great anticipation.

Brimmer then smiled. "It was a match."

Walking out of the darkness, Manning spoke. "I wouldn't have believed it!"

"Why does that not surprise me?" Walsh said. At that moment, 'Hey Jude' began playing somewhere within the camp.

"If that's truly Fred Noonan, why is his body in such good condition?" Brenda asked with a furrowed brow. "And where is Earheart's body?"

"Maybe she bailed out?" Brimmer suggested.

"She wouldn't have done that," Brenda said.

"Why not?"

"Because…" Storm continued. "Fred Noonan was not a pilot. He couldn't have kept the plane in the air."

Looking over at the plane, Walsh announced. "The fuselage doors were locked from the inside, so she had to have left the plane, and Noonan locked the door before dying in his seat."

"Maybe she left the plane after it had landed here and got lost. It happens." Walsh suggested.

Manning then said. "I think it was Mr. Mustard in the kitchen with a wrench!"

Brenda shook her head in disgust. "What?"

"It's as good of an explanation as anything else," Manning laughed.

"And what's up with all our watches going crazy simultaneously?" She asked.

Walsh held up his wrist. "And they are all back to normal again?"

Manning then questioned. "What's going on? Some kind of crazy magnetic phenomenon?"

"No," Brenda replied. "If that was the cause, they wouldn't be returning to normal most of the time."

Yadin then strolled into the light and looked down into Brenda's eyes. "Maybe it's God's hand."

"God?" Manning uttered. "What's God got to do with watches?"

Shaking his head, Yadin looked up at the fiery glow of the mountaintop above them. "I don't know, but… He is here!"

"Hogwash!" Manning said. "There's nothing here but some kind of crazy desert storm."

Walsh then jumped to Yadin's defense. "In only one spot in the entire desert?" He spoke. "Face it, Reese, something's happening here that none of us can explain! So, who's to say it's not God's hand?"

"Can we move the body tomorrow?" Brenda questioned as she looked into the fire.

"Yes!" Brimmer replied. I want to find DNA evidence for Earheart as well.

"How do you do that without a body?" Manning asked.

Brimmer folded his arms. "If we can find a strand of hair or a skin cell somewhere on the plane, that would do the trick."

Walsh nodded as Brimmer turned from the fire. "Well... I guess I'll be turning in. We have a big day ahead of us tomorrow." As he walked toward his tent, Brenda and Walsh called out with a smile.

"Goodnight." Within five minutes, both Yadin and Manning also retired to their tents.

Brenda picked up a small stick, tossed it into the dying flames, and laughed. "You know, Mr. Walsh, I'm getting used to you being around."

"Oh?" He said with a smile. "Is that a good thing?"

She smiled. "You tell me." Before he could answer, Brenda leaned over and kissed him.

Walsh smiled. "Yeah... I think it is." In the background, the Beatles song 'And I Love Her' drifted softly through the cool night air. Walsh smiled as he called out.

"Nice choice, Yadin!"

Then, from out of the darkness, Yadin replied. "Thanks!"

Laughing, Brenda turned to face Walsh again. After a moment, she reached out, covered his right eye with her palm, and nodded.

"Yep!"

Confused, Walsh pulled her hand down and inquired. "What?"

"I like you better with an eyepatch."

"Me Too!" Yadin announced from somewhere deep within his tent.

Both Brenda and Walsh called out together in frustration. "Good night, Yadin!"

"Sorry!" came the apologetic response. As they sat looking at each other, they laughed, then cuddled together in the warmth of the fire.

• • • •

Garrett Walsh stood within the plane's cargo bay and looked out the door into the night. Beyond the brightness of the campfire, he could see the large, colorful operations tent and the darkness surrounding it. Turning around, he walked to Noonan's body, which now lay beneath a white sheet, and kneeled beside it. He then pulled back the covering to reveal his peaceful face. He began wondering what this stranger's life had been like and felt a tinge of admiration and jealousy of his place in history. A place where no one else on the planet would ever get the chance to go. In his way, he had achieved the immortality Walsh had often dreamed of attaining. To his sudden shock, Noonan opened his eyes and spoke.

"I didn't believe her!"

Walsh fell backward in total horror, slamming against the back bulkhead and sliding down into a sitting position, facing the body. As he watched in disbelief, Noonan sat up.

"I had the chance, and I didn't believe her." He repeated with more conviction.

"You're dead!" Walsh announced with a furrowed brow.

"Yes, but it's not too late for you!" Noonan said as he stood upon his feet. It surprised Walsh at how strong and healthy he looked. He was a heavy-set man with short-cropped hair. He wore leather flight pants and a coat with a fur collar, making him look distinguished and in control. He walked to Walsh and offered his hand. "We must go now." In utter confusion, Walsh looked at the outstretched palm and took it into his own. Pulling him to his feet, Noonan smiled.

"Come... it's not too late."

As he followed to the door, Walsh inquired. "Too late for what?"

"Your salvation." Came the unexpected reply. Following Noonan out of the plane, he jumped to the sand and found himself standing on the edge of a rocky cliff flanked by hundreds of people dressed in robes of ancient Jerusalem. Walsh heard thunder and looked up into the gathering storm clouds that grew darker by the second. Somewhere behind them, lightning streaked across the sky. Turning to face Noonan, he asked.

"What is this place?"

He replied with one word. "Golgotha."

Walsh spun to see three crosses and a well-dressed priest standing nearby. "Ah... thou that can destroyest the temple and rebuild it in three days, save yourself and come down from the cross!"

A few feet away, another priest mocked. "He saves others, but himself he cannot save!"

"Jesus?" Walsh proclaimed to himself as he looked at the center cross. Above him, the Savor stood nailed to the wood with cold steel spikes driven through his wrists, palms, and feet. Above his head was a hand-painted sign which read 'King of the Jews'. Walsh turned to find Noonan, but he was nowhere to be seen. Within the hundreds gathered to scoff and mock Jesus, Walsh saw a small group of women dressed in simple robes. The mother of Jesus, Mary Magdalene, and Mary, the wife of Cleophas, stood crying at the horrible sight before them.

From somewhere, someone called out as they shook their fist. "If thou be the King of the Jews and Christ the chosen of God, save yourself!" As he looked around for Noonan, Walsh saw him now dressed as a Roman Centurion. He rushed forward and, with a vile laugh, spat upon the Savior. While Jesus hung in excruciating pain and anguish, he fought for breath.

He looked down at his mother and pronounced. "Woman... behold thy son." He then looked at John The Beloved and pleaded. "Behold, thy mother."

As Walsh watched with tear-filled eyes, the man hanging beside Jesus railed angrily at him. "If thou be Christ, save thyself and us!"

Hearing his words, the crucified man on the right rebuked him, saying. "Dost not thou fear God, seeing thou art in the same condemnation? And we indeed justly, for we receive the due reward of our deeds. But this man hath done nothing amiss!" He then looked at Jesus. "Lord, remember me when thou comest into thy kingdom!"

With the spirit slipping away, Jesus replied. "Verily I say unto thee, today shalt thou be with me in paradise."

"No!" Walsh screamed, but his voice was lost within the gathered mob of angry spectators and religious leaders. A man walked out of the crowd and gazed at Jesus. His eyes filled with the pain of discovering who Jesus truly was too late.

A servant of a high priest, Malchus, was with the group that had arrested Jesus the night before and had lost an ear to Simon Peter's sword. On the same night, Jesus healed him with the touch of a gentle hand. He now fell to his knees and, hiding his face, wept as the mob pushed in around him. With the loud rumble of thunder, Walsh looked up and beheld the blackness that now covered the sun. He rushed forward and began pushing through the crowd to stand before the cross.   Turning to Noonan, he pleaded. "Please... let him live!"

As he stood within his armor, Noonan laughed. "It's too late!"

With his last breath, Jesus looked up towards the heavens and spoke, "Father, into thy hands, I commend my spirit." At that moment, thunder rumbled across the sky. Falling to his knees, Walsh covered his face as the earth trembled.

The centurion standing near the cross wept as he looked up into the face of Jesus. "Truly... this was the Son of God!"

As Walsh stood, Noonan came before him with his sword drawn. "If you be a follower of Christ... you can die with him!" Shoving him backward, Walsh slipped off the cliff's edge and fell toward the rocks below. As he hurtled downward to his death, he cried out.

"Oh, God... please save me!"

"Garrett… Garrett, wake up!" Brenda called out as she continued to shake his sleeping body. She then shook him again. "Walsh! Wake up!"

"What?" He said as he woke from his nightmare. He looked up into Brenda's eyes with a sweat-soaked brow. "Wow…," He said with a smile. "Never let me fall asleep again for as long as I live!"

• • • •

Storm climbed through the open fuselage door and stood within the cargo bay, staring at the body now covered by a single white sheet. A sudden chill flowed through her body as she realized for the first time that the temperature inside the plane was colder than on the outside.

"That's odd," she announced to herself. "I wonder what's causing that?" She made her way into the cabin and, for the first time, sat in Amelia's seat. As she looked around, a strange calm fell upon her. Within the filtered sun streaming through the windows, Brenda watched dust particles drifting through the cockpit. Upon looking down in deep reverence, she placed her hands on the control wheel. In an instant, Brenda saw a vision of Amelia standing on the left wing, still dressed in the black jumpsuit and heavy leather flight jacket she wore when she left Lae, New Guinea, on July 2, 1937.

Frightened, Brenda pulled her hands away and closed her eyes. Upon opening them again a moment later, the vision had vanished. "I'm tired of seeing ghosts!" she pronounced. Shaking the image from her mind, she noticed something strange on the plane's dashboard. The onboard clock was stopped at 8:49 am. Brenda looked down at her watch and found it stopped again at 8:49 am. Having just reviewed her notes on the disappearance the night before, she recalled that Amelia's last radio communication received by the Itasca before it disappeared was at 8:43 am. Her brow furrowed as she wondered what had transpired in the following six minutes.

Looking at the remaining gauges, Brenda found them all frozen with inflight information. The altitude was one thousand feet, the outside temperature was sixty-eight degrees, and the airspeed was one hundred eighty-five miles per hour. As she looked overhead, the compass showed the plane facing north. Taping the gauge with her fingertip, she pronounced. "That's not right. This plane is facing west right now!" Realizing the impossibility, she came to the conclusion that all the readings must have frozen when the plane vanished and somehow ended up thousands of miles away.

Brenda leaned back and released a heavy sigh. So many unanswered questions were floating through her mind, and she felt overwhelmed. She closed her eyes momentarily and stepped back from all the confusion. She silently said a quick prayer and asked for clarity and understanding of the things and events happening around her. Once done, she opened her eyes and felt a prompting to gaze toward the cabin floor. There, protruding from under Amelia's seat, she saw something covered in heavy brown butcher paper. Taking it into her hand, she unwrapped it and, to her astonishment, found a fresh ham and cheese sandwich. As she held it under her nose, the wonderful aroma made her hungry. She pulled off a tiny piece of the cheese, slipped it into her mouth, and waited for her taste buds to react.

"Mmm... cheddar." She pronounced with a confused smile. "Not bad for being seventy-five years old!" Once again, she checked beneath the seat and pulled out two more unexpected items. A firm, fresh, bright red apple, and Amelia's personal journal. She opened it to a random page and stared in wonder at Amelia's thoughts written in her own hand. Each word crying out from the dust of a world long since passed. A generation now dead and left within the vaults of history to be viewed through the lens of time itself. A sudden warmth touched her heart as she felt compelled to read the first sentence.

Talked with Fred again today about Jesus Christ. Still no progress, but I'll keep praying his heart will be softened.

Brenda's brow then furrowed. Where had Amelia gone? Why was she not on the plane?

Just then, Walsh stepped up to the fuselage door and questioned. "You in here, Brenda?"

"Yeah!" she called out as she closed the book. "What's up?"

"Breakfast is almost ready." he said with a smile.

"Stay right there!" She commanded. "I have something pretty interesting to show you."

Walsh smiled as he leaned in through the open door. "Well, hurry. I'm starved!" As he stood at the door waiting, Brenda returned to the cargo bay and stood before him.

"What's so important that it couldn't wait till after breakfast… this better be good!" He questioned as he folded his arms.

"This!" Brenda said with a smile. She then held up the apple in her palm.

"An apple?"

"Not just any apple…" she began. "A seventy-five-year-old apple that is still good."

"What are you talking about?" Walsh questioned.

"Here." She then tossed it out of the plane and into his hands. "Try it!" Catching it, he held it in his open palm. Feeling it growing warmer, it grew brown within seconds.

"What kind of joke are you pulling here?" Walsh inquired. Within thirty seconds, the apple turned hot, shriveled, and then turned green with mold. Reacting, Walsh dropped it to the sand and took a step back. Brenda moved closer to the door and looked down as it turned to dust, leaving only a few dried seeds. Looking at each other in shock, they stood in silence.

"You wanna try to explain what just happened?" Walsh asked.

"I was just going to ask you the same thing," Brenda replied as she knelt in the cargo bay doorway. She then held up the sandwich. "Wanna see what happens to a ham and cheese on white bread?"

Walsh's brow furrowed. "You find that in there as well?" Brenda only nodded.

"Sure... toss it out here." When she did, it landed in the sand at Walsh's feet. Within seconds, it molded and shrank into a small green pile of dust and blew away in the soft breeze.

"Wow," Walsh uttered.

Still staring into the sand, Brenda thought momentarily and then questioned. "You remember how our watches were freaking out last night?"

"Yeah." He replied hesitantly. "What's that got to do with this?"

"I have a theory," Brenda began. "What time is it right now?" Looking down at his watch, he replied.

"7:32. Why?"

"OK... now come inside the plane." Storm requested.

As he did, Brenda stood beside him. "OK, now what?"

Storm then asked with a smile. "What time is it?"

Walsh's brow furrowed. "I just told you!"

Folding her arms, she pronounced. "Just humor me."

With deep frustration, he sighed and then looked again at his watch. The color drained from his face. "8:49."

Growing excited, Brenda then ordered. "Now... go back outside and recheck it!"

Jumping back down into the sand, he looked at his watch. "You won't believe this..."

She smiled. "I bet I will."

He then looked up into her eyes and uttered. "7:33 am."

Jumping down beside him, Brenda laughed. "I knew it!" She then grabbed Walsh by the arms and kissed him on the cheek.

"So, what does this all mean?" Walsh questioned in confusion.

"It means," Brenda said with a smile. "that, as hard as it is to believe... time is standing still on the plane!" She then added. "And it has been that way for seventy-five years!"

• • • •

"Where do you want the dead guy?" Yadin asked as he and Brimmer carried Noonan's body into the operations tent.

"Over there," Brimmer answered. "Behind the plastic sheeting." After making their way through the tent, they placed the stretcher on the small portable autopsy table and stepped back through the transparent partition.

"I'm not getting paid enough to deal with grave robbing!" Yadin uttered.

"How do you figure this is grave robbing?" Storm asked as she sat at a table looking into a microscope.

As he grew near, he said. "The way I see it... that airplane out there was suposta be that guy's tomb. He was never meant to leave it, nor was it meant to be found."

Looking up, Brenda commented. "Interesting concept." She then pushed her chair from the table and smiled. "If that were universally believed, we would know nothing about anything." She then added. "Dinosaurs, mummies, ancient civilizations..."

Yadin's brow furrowed. "Have you ever thought to consider that maybe they wouldn't have wanted to be ripped from their final resting place and paraded around in front of millions of people without their permission?" He then smiled. "Just sayin'"

Brenda nodded. "Duly noted."

As he walked into the tent, Walsh questioned, "I take it this is where the party is?"

Following close behind, Manning walked to Walsh's side. "Only if you like the smell of embalming fluid."

"OK, Howard... we're all here. What do you have for us?" Brenda questioned.

After slipping off his glasses, Brimmer blew upon them before replying. "Well... it's my professional opinion that this is Earheart's plane, and the body we found inside is indeed Fred Noonan. I found live hair follicles within the plane and ran a DNA comparison to confirm Amelia's presence. I can now say without a doubt that she was on the plane." Replacing his glasses, he then added. "But where her body is now is anyone's guess. I've also discovered small traces of gold dust residue on the back bulkhead and cargo bay floor."

Manning's interest peaked, and his eyes grew wide. "Gold? Did you say gold?"

"Yes!" Brimmer confirmed. "Probably left from gold bars being transported within the plane."

Brenda's brow furrowed in confusion. "As far as I know, there has been no mention of gold bars on this flight in any history books or conspiracy theories."

"Maybe," Brimmer added. "but they were there at one time, nevertheless."

Repeating, Manning smiled. "Gold bars?" He then questioned. "Where did they go?"

Brimmer shook his head. "I don't know. There is no way even to tell when they were there." He leaned back against a table and continued. "Brenda discovered a most interesting phenomenon while inside the plane." Looking at her, he then asked. "Will you tell them about it?"

She smiled, walked to the small group's front, and explained. "Within the plane, it's literally July 3, 1937… forever."

Manning's brow furrowed. "I don't understand."

Brenda smiled again with the excitement of Christmas morning. "Somehow, not a second has passed on that plane since the moment it disappeared on the morning of July 3, 1937, at exactly 8:49 am. Six minutes after Amelia's last received radio transmission."

Brimmer then added with a smile, "Yeah… real X-Files stuff, right?"

Manning's voice filled with anxiety. "Things like that don't happen in real life… does it?"

Brenda replied, "I've seen some weird stuff in my life, but nothing like this!"

Brimmer then spoke again. "Everything inside that plane is just as it was seventy-five years ago, down to the last dust particle. Five gallons of fuel are still left in the last auxiliary tank, and it's still useable."

Turning to face Brimmer, Yadin then asked, "What's so significant about that?"

"Normally, gas separates into its basic components within a month or two if unused. This gas hasn't done that."

Manning then pointed to Noonan's body. "Is that why the body we found hasn't decomposed yet?"

Storm smiled. "Take another look at the body now that we've taken it off the plane!" Making his way back through the plastic, he pulled the sheet back to expose Noonan's head. Shocked upon seeing Noonan's horribly decomposed face, he fell onto a table, sending all the medical equipment crashing to the ground.

"How do you explain that?" He questioned as he pulled himself back to his feet.

Brenda explained as Manning crossed through the plastic, leaving the body behind. "Outside the plane, time continues to pass for us and the rest of the world. When we brought Noonan out…"

Manning grimaced. "He rotted!"

Brimmer then said with a smile, "Yeah, you could say that."

"So… what's next?" Walsh asked as he folded his arms.

"I've got some more tests that will take the rest of the day," Brimmer replied. "I'm going to see if there is enough of Noonan left to find the cause of his death."

Yadin laughed. "I'm no expert, but consider extremely old age to be a good guess." The group erupted in laughter.

"Tomorrow, I'm going to dismantle the engines," Brenda pronounced.

"Why?" Walsh inquired.

"By exposing the engine's air filters, it can sometimes tell where the plane has been based on what it has sucked into them."

Walsh nodded. "That makes sense. I'm pretty good with car engines. Maybe I could lend a hand."

"Sounds good to me. I could use the help."

• • • •

Later that night, Walsh sat in the warmth of the campfire, reading from the Bible. In the background, 'If I Fell' from the Beatles played in Yadin's tent, followed by 'Michelle'. The music somehow helped him relax after a long day of discovery at the base of Mount Sinai. Still casting its orange glow upon the camp, the mountain loomed above them, and for the first time, Walsh felt homesick.

"Are you all right?" Brenda asked softly as she approached the fire. With a smile, Walsh placed the book on his lap and looked into her eyes. He realized how much he cared for her each time he saw her. At no other time had he ever thought about spending the rest of his life with the same woman. And yet, now, it was all he could think about. As the fire crackled before him, he replied,

"Yeah, I'm fine. Just feeling homesick right now."

Brenda moved to his side and sat down in the cool sand. "That's a new side of you I haven't seen. Where's home?"

Looking into the fire, he replied. "I've worked out of New York for the last ten years, but when I think of home, I think of Idaho."

"Were you born there?"

Walsh nodded. "Yea… I grew up on a dairy farm."

Brenda's brow furrowed. "So, why did you leave?"

Walsh took a deep breath and looked heavenward. "My father always seemed so tied down with everything… I guess I just didn't want to end up like him." He smiled. "I wanted to see the world!" Silence passed between them for a moment before he spoke again. "Now, I envy his life. He had a good wife who stuck with him through thick and thin, had a successful business doing what he loved to do, and was happy with his life."

"And you're not?"

Walsh leaned back on his hands and thought for a moment. "I used to think I was, but now," He shook his head. "I need something more in my life, something… real."

Brenda looked deeply into his eyes. "Like what?"

He took the Bible in his hands and locked eyes with hers. "This... since I've been reading it, I've been feeling things I've never felt before."

"Like what?" Brenda asked with a smile.

"I don't know for sure. Some sort of connection, maybe? The feeling that there's more to life than just me."

Brenda leaned forward. "That maybe life matters?"

"Yes!" Walsh replied. "Exactly!" He spoke, "Until now, everything seemed so… surface."

Brenda picked up a small stone and tossed it into the fire. "There is so much to know about life that most people don't even think about. Where we came from, where do we go when we die, or even the purpose of life itself?"

Watching her, Walsh repeated. "Purpose of life?"

She turned her body to face him more directly and then replied. "God created this world for us to be tested,"

In confusion, Walsh inquired. "What do you mean… tested?"

Brenda grew excited. "I believe we were born upon this earth with the challenge of finding God in our lives, to believe in Him, and then keep His commandments. We are here with the ability to use our free will to choose good or evil."

Walsh then smiled. "That seems simple enough."

"Well," Brenda said. "most people get caught up in themselves and never find the truth."

"Like I have my whole life?"

Brenda nodded. "It doesn't matter when you find the truth, but only how you act upon it once you've found it." She then added with a smile. "That's where those magical words 'repentance and forgiveness' come into play."

A sudden darkness fell upon Walsh's face as he shook his head. "I don't think those words apply to me. While working in the CIA, I've had to kill too many people. I'm probably too far gone to be forgiven."

Brenda grew serious. "Let me ask you a question. Have you ever enjoyed killing and did it without reason, or did it serve a righteous purpose?"

Walsh stared intensely into the crackling fire; his brow creased with worry. The dancing flames reflected in his somber eyes, casting a flickering glow on his troubled face. As he spoke, his voice trembled with regret. "I despise the fact that it has forced me to take lives, but it has always been in defense of myself or others," he confessed, his words heavy with remorse. "From a tender age, I felt an innate desire to shield people from harm, to be their protector." A profound silence settled over the scene, broken only by the sound of the fire. At that moment, a solitary tear escaped from his eye, tracing a path down his cheek. The tear glistened in the firelight, reflecting the pain etched on his face. Memories from the past flooded his mind, shrouding his thoughts in darkness. His stomach twisted with an anguish so profound that it threatened to consume him. His complexion turned ashen, drained of color, as the weight of the past bore down upon him.

"It started when I was twelve," he whispered, his voice barely audible. His words were laden with guilt and sorrow. "My younger brother, Jason, and I were playing ball outside. I threw it too far, and he chased after it, unaware of the danger that awaited him on the street." As he recounted the haunting event, the scene replayed in his mind like a horror film. "A van pulled up, and two men got out and took my brother away." A moment of silence passed before he could continue. "We never saw him again." His trembling hand rose to his tear-stained face, wiping away the evidence of his anguish. His gaze lifted, seeking solace in the soothing fire before him. "It was my fault," he confessed, his voice filled with self-blame. "I was supposed to be watching him, to keep him safe."

Overwhelmed with emotion, Brenda reached out and touched his arm. "Garrett, it wasn't your fault! You can't blame yourself. There was nothing you could have done to prevent it."

Walsh nodded. "I know, but… I made a vow that day that no one would ever suffer again on my watch." He then looked deeply into Brenda's eyes. "Especially those who I love!"

• • • •

Waking before the sun, Brenda had spent the first three hours of the new day going through the many systems of the Electra. Her primary focus being electrical, fuel lines, navigation systems, and communications. She had hoped to be finished by the time Walsh was up and ready to work on the engines and had been successful in her goal. She now sat in the cockpit with Amelia's journal in her hands.

With the morning sun came a warmth through the windows that fell upon her face. She closed her eyes and, for a moment, cleared her mind of the still unanswered questions plaguing her thoughts. The soft sound of her stomach growling brought her back into focus on the book before her. Opening the first page, she read.

June 1, 1937

Had breakfast with GP this morning before beginning my circumnavigational flight around the world. I can't express the excitement I feel about my dream coming true. Having George with me this morning eased any reservations I had about this flight. He is such a supportive husband and friend. We talked about the flight and expressed our love for each other. He also told me his son George from his first wife Dorthy could not join us in California upon my return. I know how much GP loves his two sons. I feel the need to give him children of our own and I confess, the Idea of having a daughter is delightful, but I have a hard time seeing myself as a mother.

-A.E.

Placing the open journal upon her lap, her mind recalled Amelia's words that now struck home. She repeated the words from memory.

"The idea of having a daughter is delightful." As she turned, she looked out the left window again and saw Amelia standing on the wing, but she was not alone this time. Beside her now was Brenda's daughter, Rose. With a gasp, her hand flew to her mouth as tears of joy fell from her eyes. Breathing in, she closed her eyes as years passed away, and a precious memory returned to her mind:

"You have to be quiet, mommy…" Brenda's six-year-old daughter whispered as her mother walked into the room. "Nemo is sleeping!" As Brenda drew near, she gazed into a small fish bowl in her daughter's hands and saw her large pet goldfish floating upon the water's surface. Brenda's heart melted as she looked into Rose's eyes. She had spoken with her husband, Michael, only a week before about when it would be appropriate to explain death to their daughter. When her grandmother died, she asked questions, and now the job had fallen into Brenda's lap. She knelt before Rose and stroked her hair. "Nemo's not sleeping!" She spoke.

"He's not? Then why is he not moving?" Rose questioned with tiny furrowed brows.

"Well, sweetheart," Brenda began. "Nemo has gone to Heaven to live with Jesus."

Rose looked into the bowl and shook her head. "No, he's not… he's right there!"

Brenda chuckled. "His body is still there, but his spirit has gone to heaven."

Looking back into the bowl, confusion filled her childish face. "I don't understand mommy!"

Brenda smiled, took the bowl, and placed it on the tabletop. She pulled Rose onto her lap as they sat together on the floor. She put her fingertip on Rose's chest.

"Your spirit is what's inside of your body… here. It's the thoughts you think, the love you feel, and what makes your body move and talk." Brenda smiled and, holding her hands up, wiggled her fingers.

"Now… do this." Rose giggled and repeated the action. Brenda touched her uplifted hand and pronounced with a smile. "Pretend this is your spirit," she began. "It's all the things that make you… you." She then lowered her hand slowly. "Your spirit comes down when you are born." Quickly looking around her room, she picked up a mitten from the floor and began slipping it onto Rose's outstretched hand. "Our spirits then go into our baby bodies like this." Brenda then whispered, "Wiggle your fingers again." Laughing, Rose obeyed. Brenda then walked her fingers across the carpet in front of her. "We grow up, attend school, get married, and live happily." Rose then copied her action. "And then something wonderful happens," Brenda pronounced with a smile.

"What?" Rose questioned.

Pulling the mitten from her hand, she laid it on the floor and lifted Rose's hand back into the air. "We die, and our spirits leave our bodies and go to live with Jesus in Heaven."

"Like Grandma?" Rose asked in a whisper.

Nodding, Brenda answered, "Yep." She then leaned closer as she asked, "But do you know what's special?"

"What?"

"When we all go to Heaven, we get to be together forever!"

Rose giggled with joy and clapped her hands. "Yea!"

At that moment, Michael walked through the front door and called out, "I'm home! Is anyone else here?"

"Daddy!" Rose called out as she jumped up and headed for the sound of her father's voice. Within seconds, she was in his arms.

As Brenda joined them in the living room, she smiled. "Hi, sweety!" She stood at the door frame and watched the interaction with amusement.

"Daddy... guess what?" Rose asked as she took her father's face in both tiny hands.

"What, love bug?"

"Nemo died today, and his spirit went to Heaven to live with Grandma until we can all be together again!" Michael looked into Brenda's eyes with confusion.

"Sounds like you had... the talk."

Smiling, Brenda replied, "Yeah, the next one is your turn."

Michael laughed as he looked back into Rose's face. "Well then, how would you and Mommy like to go out and get an ice cream cone?"

Rose nodded. "Only if I can take Chester with us. He's part of our family, too, you know!" Michael laughed as he sat her down.

Michael took Brenda into his arms as Rose returned to her room to get her teddy bear. "I'm so blessed to spend the rest of my life with you!"

With tears of joy and great gratitude, Brenda asked for something that would never be fulfilled. "Just promise me something…"

Kissing her, he said with a smile. "Anything!"

She placed her arms around his neck and smiled. "Promise that you'll never leave me!" He then kissed her again and smiled. "I Promise!"

As she opened her eyes slowly, the memory faded. Brenda once again sat alone in Earheart's plane, and a sudden deep depression fell upon her as she remembered that less than an hour later, a tragic accident would tear her family away from her, changing her life forever. The thought struck hard at her heart. Without noticing, when her tears had fallen, she spotted the pages of Amelia's journal, which was still open on her lap. She turned, looked out the window again, and saw Rose standing on the wing. Not realizing she had been holding her breath, she exhaled as she tried to stifle a great sob. Upon wiping her eyes, Rose vanished.

"Are you all right?" Walsh questioned as his head appeared in the cabin crawlspace.

Surprised by his voice, Brenda spun around to face him and faked a small smile. "Yeah… I'm OK."

Walsh smiled. "You know that you're becoming a better liar than me."

She chuckled as she wiped the newest tears from her cheeks. "Sorry."

"You wanna talk about it?" Walsh offered with genuine concern in his voice.

Smiling, she then shook her head. "Maybe later." Hoping to see Rose again, she glanced back out the window but saw nothing. She turned back to Walsh and asked. "How did this plane get here?"

Shaking his head, he replied, "Well… it didn't have enough fuel to fly this far-off course, that's for sure!"

"No!" Brenda proclaimed. "I mean in this pocket canyon! It's only two hundred and ten feet from one side to the other. There is no way it could have landed here like a conventional aircraft!"

Walsh looked up to the high cliffs all around them and then said, "It's like the plane has been…"

Brenda finished his sentence. "Placed here by the very hand of God?" Staring into each other's eyes, Walsh nodded. Looking up to the cliff before them, Brenda saw Jehorum and his female companion from the Guardians of the Exodus watching from atop their black horses. "And why are they so concerned with this airplane? It's got nothing to do with Moses or the Exodus!"

"Maybe they're just worried that we're this close to Mount Sinai?" Walsh guessed.

Brenda's head shook. "I don't think that's the reason. There's got to be something else keeping them here. Something we don't know about!"

Walsh laughed. "There are many things we don't know about right now!" He then looked up. "They have not tried to stop us. I don't think they see us as a danger."

"Not yet, anyway." Storm replied. Turning to face him, she questioned with a smile. "You ready to tear an engine apart and see if it holds any answers to the three thousand questions we already have?"

"You know… this could open a whole new can of worms, right?"

While Brenda moved toward him, she chuckled.

"Yeah… that's what I'm afraid of!"

• • • •

An Unexpected Turn of Events

Inside the operations tent, Brenda sat before a wall of laptop screens and scanning equipment, verifying the information they had recovered from the engine air filter. In a typical operation, investigators would look into the cause of a crashed aircraft when no apparent reason was found. After checking her records and internet resource information, she leaned back in her chair and exhaled.

"Find anything of interest?" Walsh asked as he entered the tent.

"Yeah… you could say that!" Brenda leaned forward, picked up something with a small pair of tweezers, and held it out for Walsh to see. "What do you think this is?" She asked with a smile.

Looking closely, he guessed, "A pretty pink dragonfly?"

"Exactly!" she answered.

"So… that means what?" Walsh questioned with a furrowed brow.

"Have you ever seen a fluorescent pink dragonfly?" Brenda asked as she leaned back in her folding chair.

"No… not in real life."

"Well," Brenda began. "neither has anyone else on this planet!"

Walsh's eyes narrowed. "What do you mean?"

With a smile, she replied, "I mean… this dragonfly species doesn't exist."

"Of course it does." He pointed to it in her hand and spoke. "It's right there!" Brenda returned the specimen to its place under the microscope and smiled.

Walking in, Brimmer drew near the table and nodded. "She's right, you know, this dragonfly has an unidentifiable DNA structure I've never seen before."

Walsh scratched his head, "So, tell me what that means in English." Brenda folded her arms and repeated, "It means this dragonfly species does not exist. Anywhere on this planet!"

Walsh stood silently for a moment as he looked from face to face and then said. "You guys are pulling my leg, right?" Both replied by shaking their heads. Brenda pulled out another small container and dumped its continence upon a white paper.

"And then there's this."

Leaning over, Walsh looked closer. "What is it?"

Brimmer picked it up and placed it into Walsh's hand. "This... is an apple blossom."

"OK... so what?" Walsh questioned with a smirk.

Brenda said, "By doing tests and finding information in the FDA database, we've concluded that there is only one place in the world where this particular blossom can be found." With a smile, Brenda questioned, "Guess where that is?"

Walsh's eyebrows arched. "I don't know!"

Brimmer then pronounced. "Atchison, Kansas!"

"So? What's so significant about that?"

In disgust, Brenda questioned. "Didn't you do any background research on Amelia before you joined our little band?"

"Well, I..." Walsh began.

Cutting him off, Brenda then said. "Atchison, Kansas is the birthplace of Amelia Earheart."

"Is that suposta mean something to me?" Walsh asked.

"Only the fact that this plane has never flown anywhere near Kansas on her flight might make it strange, don't you think?" Brenda asked with folded arms.

"So, if that's true... how did it come to be stuck in the air filter?" He questioned.

"That, my friend," she pronounced. "Is the million-dollar question."

• • • •

An hour later, with his back turned from the door, Yadin sat in his tent, reviewing the song list on his MP3 player. Entering the tent, Manning made his way to stand behind him. He pulled out a gun and commanded. "Turn around, kid!"

Yadin jumped in surprise and then spun to face him. "What's going on?" He asked.

"It's time for all the fun and games to end."

"It's you!" Yadin exclaimed. "You're the Blue Meanie!"

Manning's brow furrowed. "Yeah, whatever!"

"What are you going to do?" Yadin asked as he stood to face him.

"Kill them all!" Manning said.

Yadin felt a sudden icy chill flow over his body as he asked, "What about me?"

Manning said, "I'll need you to get me back to Cairo." He waved his gun and then said. "Now, be a nice young man, turn around, and put your hands behind your back." After complying, Manning tied his hands and gagged him. "I wish I could kill you as well… you and that horrible music you've been playing from those no-talent hacks you so dearly love!" Yadin's brow furrowed as he tried to speak. Manning struck him on the head with his gun and watched as he fell to the ground. "When I'm done with the others, I'll return for you!" He then walked to the opening of the supply tent and slipped in unnoticed. He found the dynamite and, taking one in his hand, made his way into the camp where Brenda, Walsh, and Brimmer were now sitting. Then, lighting the long fuse, he pulled out his gun and called from behind them. "Everyone, drop your guns!"

The group spun around to face him in surprise. "Manning?" Walsh asked. "It was you all along?"

"Yeah, it was me!" He spoke. "Too bad you found out a bit too late. Now, throw down your guns!" Brenda and Walsh complied.

"Why are you doing this?" Brenda questioned in confusion.

"Isn't it obvious?" He said with a smile. "Someone else wants the credit for this discovery!"

"Feisali?" Brimmer questioned.

Manning laughed. "Among others." The tension in the air grew palpable as their conversation continued.

"Now it's time for all of you to die!" Manning exclaimed, his voice filled with malice. His finger tightened on the trigger, aiming directly at Brenda's head. "Goodbye, Storm, it's been fun!"

In anticipation of the bullet, Brenda gripped Walsh's hand, feeling its warmth and reassurance. She closed her eyes and waited for the gun to discharge. Time stood still as Brenda waited in confusion. She slowly opened one eye, only to find Manning frozen, his vacant gaze fixed ahead. Then, slowly, he dropped to his knees and collapsed face-first into the sandy ground. It was then that they noticed the arrow lodged in his back. Looking beyond Manning's' body, Yadin stood with his bow in hand. Walsh wasted no time, lunging forward to seize the dynamite, feeling its weight in his hand. He swiftly hurled it as far away as possible.

"Get down!" he bellowed, throwing himself into the sand and covering his head. A thunderous explosion erupted, sending the sand into the air like a storm before descending in a gentle shower. Rising to his feet, Walsh patted Yadin's back.

"Great shooting!"

"Well... not really," Yadin said with a grimace. "I was aiming for his arm!" His brow then furrowed in anger. "Although, he had the nerve to call the Beatles no talent hacks!"

••••

"Hey guys!" Brimmer said as he stood above the enormous crater in the sand left by the explosion. "Come, take a look at this."

Yadin ran to his side, looked down into the hole, and blew a soft whistle. "Wow!"

"What is it?" Brenda asked as she and Walsh drew near.

"You're the expert on ancient history, you tell us," Brimmer said. Once on the brink of the crater, she looked down. Below them, the explosion had exposed what looked like a manufactured floor of carved stone blocks sitting four feet below the sand.

"What is that?" Yadin asked as he stepped down to its edge. "Some kind of ancient road?"

Brenda shook her head in reply. "Don't know." She then made her way to its edge and knelt. Reaching out, she ran her finger along one crack between the stones.

Yadin took three steps out into its center and stopped. Jumping up and down, he laughed. "Someone sure knew how to build sturdy roads back then." Without notice, the block he stood upon gave way beneath his feet. Yadin screamed as he fell into the dark oblivion below.

"Yadin!" Storm called out as she watched him disappear before her eyes. As sand and ancient dust billowed up from inside the hole, she saw his fingertips clinging to the edge of the remaining stones. "Yadin!" she called again in anguish. Walsh moved forward and, grabbing his wrists, pulled him to safety.

"Are you all right?" Brenda asked as she moved beside him.

Yadin then smiled. "I take it this isn't a road!"

"Apparently not." She said with a laugh. "Unless they used to have extremely large gophers the size of water buffalos!"

"OK...So if that's not a road, what is it?" Brimmer asked in confusion.

Brenda returned to the edge and looked down into the darkness. "We won't know unless I go down there and find out."

Walsh's head snapped up. "Wait, a minute... I don't think that's such a good idea!"

Brenda quickly spun to face him. "Garrett, that's my job! I'm an anthropologist. I study the unknown!"

His brow furrowed. "But this could be dangerous!" He looked down into the hole and spoke, "We don't know what's down there. What if it's filled with snakes?"

Benda smiled. "You've been watching way too many Indiana Jones movies! Taking chances and pushing yourself past your natural limits sets people apart. Most people go through life doing nothing that challenges them and always staying safe. Just existing and nothing more!" She then smiled. "You should know by now that I'm not that kind of person." She then stood. "Now, if you want to go with me, I'd love the company." She then turned to Brimmer and Yadin. "Any of you want to go as well?"

Brimmer took three steps back and shook his head. "No... I hate snakes!"

Walsh smiled as he stood beside her. "I'll go get us some rope and the lanterns." Tying one end of the rope to the plane's landing gear, Walsh tossed it into the hole and turned to face Brenda. He pulled out his gun and spun its chamber.

With a smile, she asked, "Feeling macho?" She then laughed. "Now, I suppose you want to go in first to ensure it's safe for poor little me?"

Replacing his gun, he took the rope into his hands and sat on the hole's edge. "Yes!" was his only reply.

"Oh, goodie! I feel so safe!" she said to herself. Looking into his eyes, she continued. "I've been doing this for years without your protection!"

As Walsh began lowering himself into the hole, he smiled. "The monsters are bigger here!"

As he watched from the edge, Brimmer questioned. "Monsters?"

"Don't worry, Howard," Storm replied, lowering herself into the hole. "Rambo Walsh here will protect us all."

Walsh's voice echoed through the room as he exclaimed, "I heard that!"

Storm descended from above, stepping onto the stone block floor. She raised her lantern, illuminating the stagnant air that hung around them. The dust, ancient and untouched for two thousand years, drifted lazily, defying the pull of gravity like tiny raindrops. Inclosing them were unyielding stone walls, while a massive round stone pillar stood proudly in the center, reaching six feet.

"What on earth is that?" Walsh asked as he held his lantern closer.

As she drew near, Brenda looked up into the light and exhaled. "Wow!" Perched on the pillar, a white stone skull with piercing red ruby eyes overlooked the surroundings. The precious stone eyes glowed with pure evil with the lantern's movement.

"Eyes of Ningal," Brenda uttered as she drew closer.

"Eyes of who?" Walsh asked.

Examining what was before them, Brenda spoke, "In early Mesopotamian mythology, the God Sin was married to the Goddess Ningal. Some believe the eyes are a reminder of eventual judgment."

"So… are we going to take them back with us? They must be worth a small fortune!" Suddenly, the earth shook, causing dust and sand to fall from the ceiling.

"I'm going to take that as a solid no!" She then saw something within her light. Brenda moved to the north wall and stood before a large stone tablet resting on a platform.

"Can you read what that says?" Walsh asked as he drew to her side. Brenda nodded as she turned her focus on the engraved writing. "It's the Sin Creation Myth."

Walsh then questioned, "Well… what does it say?"

She stepped closer and read. "The sun God Sin was the son of the sky, God Encil, and the grain Goddess Ninlil. It says that when Ninlil was bathing in the sacred river, Encil saw her and was filled with lust and seduced her. Because of what he did, the God Marduk banished him to the Netherworld. Because Ninlil was now pregnant, she went with him. Once the baby was born, they gave Sin the title of Moon God and banished him to the Underworld, where he rules to this day."

"Pleasant Life!" Walsh said with a glance into Brenda's eyes.

Looking around again, Brenda asked. "Do you know what this means?"

Walsh smiled. "That I should stay away from naked girls in rivers?" Brenda's brow furrowed. "Is it possible for you to be serious for even a second?"

Humbled, he replied. "Sorry."

"It means we are standing in the middle of a Paleolithic Sanctuary of Sin!" Brenda then explained in a reverent tone. "It's where earthly worshipers gathered together to offer sacrifice to him."

Walsh pulled out his gun and whispered. "Human?"

Brenda laughed. "Take it easy, big boy…" She pushed down his gun and continued. "Something has buried this place for the last two millennia. No one else even knows it's here." He replaced his weapon and followed Brenda through an arched passageway into a much larger room. On the walls hung ancient torches that were once used to illuminate the chamber. He walked to the closest one and, pulling out his lighter, put it to the torch. It sputtered for only a moment before coming to life.

"That's better!" He pronounced as he pulled it from the wall and walked to the next one. Then, repeating the process, the room became visible. Along opposite side walls, eight large stone sarcophaguses stood facing each other, making both visitors uneasy. Brenda walked to face one and touched it with her outstretched palm.

"What is this place?" Walsh questioned as he drew near to her side.

"It's the burial chamber," She whispered in reply.

"For who?"

Brenda turned to face him. "This was the dwelling place of Sin. It served as a bridge between the sky and the earth. To be more specific, the Underworld." She slowly ran her hand across the cold white stone and continued. "For over four millennia, early Akkadian Kings appointed their mothers and daughters as high priestesses of Sin. When they died, they were sealed up within these temples to serve him in the Netherworld."

After Looking over his shoulder, Walsh said, "This Sin guy must have been pretty important!"

Brenda nodded. "His followers consider Sin to be the Lord of all wisdom." She turned to face him. "He is the keeper of time and guardian of all humanity."

"That's a lot of responsibility to put on one man."

"Sin's not a man," she said as she spun to face him. "He's a God!" Walsh replied. "Whatever!"

Growing deeply concerned, Brenda then took a step toward him.

"Don't mock what you don't understand, Garrett! His power is real. Most myths have some basis, in fact, somewhere down the line."

Walsh pulled out his gun and held it up. "I have found no myths or ancient monsters that this couldn't take care of!"

Brenda's brow furrowed. "You have no clue!" She took another step closer to him and looked deeply into his eyes. "I've heard stories…"

"Exactly!" Walsh interrupted. "Just stories… that's all they are, Brenda! Just Stories!" He replaced his gun and then walked away. Within the center of the chamber, a large flat stone shaped like a crescent moon stood upon a slab of dark rock. The raised platform was three feet in height. As Walsh neared it, he asked.

"What's this?"

Brenda turned and walked to his side. "It's an altar to Sin. Anciently, it was called a Galed. A place of worship and sacrifice." She reached down and touched it. "The crescent moon is the symbol that represents Sin."

Walsh ran his fingers across the blackened center of the top stone. "Looks like it's been burned."

Brenda nodded. "Legends say that the early followers burned their sacrifices alive.

"Ouch!" Walsh replied. "Hopefully, they weren't human sacrifices!"

"Don't know for sure," Brenda pronounced. "but I have known it to happen with the followers of Sin in modern times."

"Modern Times? You're telling me this guy still has followers?"

Storm nodded her head and then added. "Satan has a way of corrupting religions even now." She then turned around and held her torch high to light the back of the chamber. She was shocked by what stood before her. Her heart began racing, and she had to fight to keep breathing.

When the blood drained from her face, Walsh asked, "What's the matter?"

"Do you know what that is?" She then asked. Against the back wall, a large white stone platform stood with a six-foot high rough-hewn wooden stick protruding from it. Around the middle, a dirty cloth strip hung down from the center.

"A tree branch?" Walsh answered with a smug smile.

"That…" she replied in awe. "Is the staff of Moses!"

"So, how do you know that?" Walsh questioned as he took a step toward it.

"The new scrolls that were found describe it perfectly." She then pointed. "And that's it!" As he neared the stone, Walsh reached out to touch it. The earth shook again as small stones and dust fell into the chamber, filling it with a fine brown mist.

"Don't touch it!" Brenda screamed as she grabbed Walsh's arm. "It's not worth our lives." The rumbling then stopped. Both stood staring at the most unattainable treasure of all time. "The only thing that would be more exciting to find would be the Ark of the Covenant!" Brenda exclaimed. "And God won't even let us touch this."

Walsh nodded. "If that thing holds God's power within it, who knows what it could be capable of?"

A voice then called out from behind them. "Exactly! That's what I'm counting on."

Brenda Spun around. "Foster… why am I not surprised to see you here?" With a gun, Sigman Foster walked out of the darkness and into the chamber with Feisali close behind.

"Oh, look…" Walsh said. "It's Humpty and Dumpty!" He smiled and then added, "Hey, Feisali… Is your nose feeling any better?"

"Shut up!" Feisali screamed as he stuck his gun into Walsh's face.

Foster smiled. "Nice to see you again, lass. I came for Earheart's plane, but you've given me a much grander prize. Glad you could do my work for me again. You're getting superb at it."

Brenda nodded. "Don't mention it."

Foster's brogue brought a smile to Walsh's face. He then questioned, "You know this Scottish skunk?"

Foster turned to face him. "Aye, Laddie, Dr. Storm, and I be old friends."

Walsh folded his arms and grinned. "Well, there's no accounting for some people's taste!"

Foster held up his gun. "Now be a good lad and toss down any weapons you may be concealing! Walsh stepped back and complied with the request, "Now yours as well, my bonnie lass." Brenda glanced at Walsh and then complied. Foster walked to Moses's staff and stopped. "It be a grand sight, is it not?" Feisali spun to face Foster and raised his gun on him.

"I didn't travel all the way from Cairo to stare at some worthless tree branch. I'm here to raise Sin and his priestesses from the Netherworld!"

"Are you crazy?" Storm asked.

"I've been searching for this temple for ten years, and you've brought it right to me. What an unexpected turn of events."

Walsh turned to Storm and whispered, "Can he do that?"

She nodded and replied, "Only if he holds the E-Temen-Nigur scroll of Giparu."

Walsh's brow furrowed. "The what?"

"Basically," she began. "It's a scroll found in the ruins of Qumran in 1947 that holds the ancient instructions for raising the dead." She then turned back to Feisali. "Sin worshipers have been trying to get their hands on it forever!"

Holding a wrapped roll of parchment, Feisali laughed, "Not anymore!" Foster turned his gun in hand. "I wouldn't do that if I were you! Put it down. Now!" Feisali shouted. "I have no desire to kill you as well!" Foster reluctantly tossed his gun to the ground.

"Now, shall we begin?" Feisali asked as he then climbed upon the white stone altar.

Brenda bit her lip and then questioned. "Have you read all the instructions on that scroll?"

Feisali laughed, "Of course I have. Do you think me a fool?"

She raised one eyebrow. "You really want to know?"

Walsh backed away with the torch still in his hands. He then turned back to Brenda and whispered. "He can't really do that… can he?"

As he held the unrolled scroll, Feisali began to read, "Oh, great and powerful Marduk, the true king of the heavens and the Netherworld. I come in praise of your name and ask of you a blessing. Narasta barlok pastano ella haum. Release Sin, the God of the moon, and his servants, so they may again take their place among

Sin's followers!" At that instant, Walsh spun around as the eight sarcophaguses along the walls began shaking. The four-thousand-year-old dust and dirt drifted to the stones beneath their feet as he watched. An ear-splitting shriek pierced the silence, causing Walsh to wince in pain.

"Rise!" Feisali commanded. "Be free of your bonds of the Netherworld and walk again amongst the living!" The force of his words seemed to conjure a storm as the lids of the coffins exploded open. Before them stood the grotesque remains of the priestesses, their mummified bodies quivering with otherworldly energy, clutched in their withered hands were weapons of death, a chilling reminder of their past deeds. Brenda shivered as the temperature dropped sixty degrees in a matter of seconds. Feisali's voice changed into something dark and horrifying as his eyes glowed red.

"Yes, yes! Rise to serve your master!" The mummies stepped from their resting places and stumbled forward. The air filled with the putrid smell of ancient rotting flesh.

Taking another step backward, Walsh looked at Brenda. "I think we're in a tiny bit of doo-doo about now!"

Brenda's brow furrowed. "Doo-doo? That's what you call this? Yeah, you could say that!" she replied in disgust.

As the living dead moved toward them, Feisali dropped his gun, raised both of his hands above his head and screamed, "Kill them, kill them all!" The chilling command reverberated through the chamber. In that ominous moment, a mummy, shrouded in ancient bandages, lunged forward with a long spear, driving it mercilessly through Feisali's body. The sickening sound of flesh being pierced and the metallic smell of blood filled the room. Feisali, now on his knees on the altar, gasped for his final breath, his voice strained with betrayal.

"I brought you back to life, and this is how you repay me?" he questioned.

Brenda, standing nearby, responded with amusement, "I take it you didn't bother to read the fine print in the instructions?" she asked, shaking her head in disappointment. "It requires a sacrifice upon the altar. That would be you!" As Feisali's lifeless body slumped onto the cold stone, the scroll slipped from his grasp, its ancient secrets exposed. In a swift motion, Storm retrieved her guns from the ground. She unleashed a barrage of gunfire at the advancing undead horde, the loud echoes bouncing off the cavernous walls. The bullets tore through the decaying flesh, leaving no lasting impact. Armed with a torch, Walsh swung it wildly at the encroaching mummies, the flames casting eerie shadows across the room.

"Burn the scroll!" Storm urgently called out, her voice drowned out by the cacophony of shrieks and moans.

Confusion etched on Walsh's face, he shouted in response, "What did you say?"

Hearing his bewildered cry, Brenda repeated, her voice stern and determined, "I said... burn the scroll!" As Brenda retreated, her movements hurried and panicked; she stumbled and fell to the cold floor. Three mummies closed in, their ancient weapons poised to strike. In a desperate attempt to save himself, Walsh set one priestess ablaze with his torch. Turning to Storm, his brow furrowed.

"I don't think this is the time to clean up our messes!" With her last two bullets, Brenda aimed and fired at the nearest mummy. The creature, seemingly unfazed, took a menacing step forward, raising its spear high, ready to deliver a fatal blow.

Fueled by desperation, Brenda's voice cracked with hysterical urgency. "Just do it!" she screamed, her eyes tightly shut, bracing herself for her impending doom. In a moment of realization, Walsh's gaze fell upon the scroll, its ancient power pulsating. Rolling swiftly, he brought his torch in contact with the fragile papyrus, igniting a fierce blaze that consumed it within seconds. The scent of burning parchment filled the chamber as the ancient scroll turned to ash. When Brenda opened her eyes, the last two attacking mummies disintegrated into fine dust, drifting down to settle upon the stone floor. The chamber, once filled with menacing figures, now stood empty. Approaching Brenda, Walsh extended his hand and helped her to her feet, their bodies trembling with adrenaline and relief.

"Can we please go home now?" He questioned with a smile. "I've had quite enough excitement for one day."

Picking up his gun, Foster moved to face them. "Aye, laddie, tis' time to be going." He drew near the staff and spoke. "But we be takin' this little trinket with us!"

Taking a step forward, Brenda pronounced. "Don't touch it, Foster!" She then added. "I'm warning you."

As he took another step closer, Foster said. "I think you forgot who has the upper hand here, Dr. Storm." His fingers grazed its smooth surface as he reached for the staff, sending a shiver down his spine. "You're in no position to be telling me what to do." The chamber quaked wrathfully when his hand closed around the staff, causing Brenda's heart to stop. She looked up, her eyes widening in horror as the chamber's walls crumbled inward, a symphony of crashing stone filling the air.

"Foster, let it go!" she cried out, her voice barely audible over the growing rumble. But Foster's face contorted with anger and an insatiable greed that twisted his features.

"It's mine! It's mine, I tell you!" he bellowed, his voice echoing through the crumbling chamber. Huge chunks of stone tumbled around them, threatening to crush them as Foster forcefully pulled the staff from its resting place.

Brenda locked eyes with him, her desperate plea echoing in her voice. "Let it go... now!"

Holding the staff aloft, its ethereal blue glow enveloping him, Foster's body radiating with power. A scream tore through the air as he slammed the staff's end into the sandy ground, declaring,

"I command the power of God!"

Amidst the earth-shaking rumble, Walsh and Storm heard stone grinding upon stone. The ceiling above them crumbled, and Walsh instinctively spun towards the doorway. Panic seized him as a massive stone slab began to descend and seal their only escape. Rushing to Brenda's side, Walsh desperately grasped her hand. "We have to get out of here... now!" he shouted, his voice mixed with fear and determination.

Brenda resisted, turning to face Foster with tear-filled eyes. "Is there nothing else we can do to help him?

Walsh's head shook, sadness and resignation etched on his face, "It's too late, Brenda... he's made his choice. We can't save him now." Tears streamed down Brenda's face as she struggled with the weight of the situation. The earth continued to tremble as Walsh's voice grew urgent, "Come on!" he shouted, his grip tightening on her hand. They sprinted towards the opening, their lives hanging by a thread. They slid under the closing slab with seconds to spare, leaving Foster trapped inside. Dust billowed, and stones rained down as they ascended the rope, gasping for breath. They collapsed on a small hill, their bodies trembling, as they watched the underground sanctuary of Sin collapse and vanish into oblivion. What lay within it, buried for time and all eternity.

Between heavy breaths, Walsh then said. "It's too bad nothing exciting ever happens to you!"

Brenda smiled. "What can we do for fun, then?"

Walsh leaned over and kissed her. "Oh... I'm sure we could find something to do." A strange sound behind them drew their attention. They both turned to see Brimmer and Yadin tied and gagged against the operations tent. Looking back at each other, Walsh asked, "You think we should let them go?" Yadin's brow furrowed as he mumbled something unrecognizable.

Brenda smiled. "I don't know. It's been nice not hearing any Beatles' music!"

Walsh then added. "And I believe we've paid the boy far too much. He then leaned over and kissed her again. "And it's nice to have some time alone."

Brenda questioned, "So... how much more time do you think we need?"

Thinking a moment, Walsh smiled, "How about another week?" Yadin then began struggling to get free as his eyebrows arched. Watching him, Walsh laughed, "Maybe two."

• • • •

The Choice

Walking into the operations tent, Yadin found Storm trying to read Earheart's journal as she lifted a fresh cup of herbal tea to her lips. With her recent encounter within the temple, she was still struggling with her thoughts about Foster's and Feisali's death and finding it hard to focus. Her anger and resentment toward them had vanished, and now all she felt was compassion. Then, her mind shifted to Rose and Michael. She remembered the sweet reunion at the Yacasum Oasis and everything Michael and Rose had said about forgiveness. Now, she could tell that she was free from that bondage and felt a sudden wave of joy flow through her body.

After meeting Walsh, she knew now that there was still room within her heart for love. She didn't need to pretend anymore that she didn't need someone in her life. She had come full circle and was ready for whatever came next.

"We've got company," Yadin said as he drew near.

Rising from the table, Storm asked. "Who is it?"

"Jehorum and his friend."

With a smile, she responded, "Why does that not surprise me?" She opened the tent flap and entered the twilight with Yadin close behind. Hearing them approaching, Walsh and Brimmer joined them. As they watched, the riders reined their beautiful black stallions to a halt before them.

"I take it you saw what happened?" Brenda asked.

"You must leave!" Jehorum commanded.

Walsh took a step forward. "If this is about that little... incident earlier today, it wasn't our fault."

"You must leave," Jehorum repeated as he leaned forward on his mount. "For the Lord has commanded it."

Walsh's brow furrowed. "Well... about that."

With sudden urgency, Jehorum interrupted, "Now!"

Brenda then took a step to join Walsh. "Wait, a minute," she began. "All we are trying to do here is get some answers about Amelia Earheart!" As she turned to face the plane, she added. "How and why did her plane come to be here, and what happened to her?"

After climbing down from her horse, the woman rider said. "Maybe I can answer some of your questions." Brenda recognized her voice as American and starkly contrasted with Jehorum's accent.

Jehorum frowned from atop of his horse. "This is not a wise choice of action!"

Looking up at him, the woman replied. "Lighten up... what harm could it do? If they say anything, no one will believe them, anyway."

Walsh then questioned, "What's going on here?"

They watched as the mystery woman pulled off her veil and head wrap and fluffed her short, shaggy brown hair. She turned around and walked forward with an extended hand, proclaimed with a smile.

"Hi, my name is Amelia Earheart!" Brenda's eyes widened as she saw Amelia approach. With shaky knees, Brenda reached out and clasped Amelia's hand in hers, feeling a surge of disbelief.

"You're... Amelia Earheart?" she stammered, her voice barely audible.

Brimmer's brow furrowed in disbelief, his breath escaping in a hushed exclamation, "No way!"

Unable to contain his astonishment, Walsh took a hesitant step forward. "That's totally impossible!" he pronounced.

Amelia chuckled softly, her laughter filling the air. "Well, Mr. Walsh, if it's impossible... how do you explain me?"

Brenda, still in a state of disbelief, dared to ask once more. "You're... THE Amelia Earhart?"

Amelia nodded, a genuine smile lighting up her face. "In the flesh," she replied. "Well... kind of." She paused for a moment, her expression thoughtful. "An updated version of me, anyway." As

Brenda absorbed this astonishing revelation, she couldn't help but notice the lightness and friendliness in Amelia's voice, a stark contrast to what she had expected from someone of such significance. A whirlwind of questions flooded Brenda's mind, and she glanced over at Walsh, seeking confirmation. "So... if you are Earheart, how did you get here, and how come you haven't aged in seventy-five years?" Brenda inquired, her curiosity overwhelming her.

Amelia's smile grew more comprehensive, and she gently took Brenda's hands in hers. "Great question!" Amelia exclaimed. "If you want to know the answer, we should all sit down. This is going to take a while."

"Yes, please!" Brenda replied.

After sitting, Amelia began, "On the morning of July 2, 1937, Fred and I were desperately searching for Howland Island on the last leg of our flight as our fuel and hope were running low." As Amelia spoke, she took the group back through time with her story:

"I suggest we not fly into that thing, whatever it is." Fred Noonan said as the light before them grew brighter.

Nodding, Amelia gripped the wheel. "I'd have to agree with you on this one, Fred!" As she attempted to change direction, she found the wheel and rudder unusable. "I can't change direction. We're goin' in!" Everything in Amelia's sight turned white after the blinding light filled the cockpit. Opening her eyes, she stood alone within a large apple orchard that looked vaguely familiar. The plane sat behind her, but she saw no sign of Noonan. She noticed the odd color of the sky. Instead of being blue, it was a vivid shade of turquoise with drifting clouds of azure.

"Hello, Millie," A soft voice called from behind her. Amelia spun around with surprise and stood before an older man in an oversized gray business suit and fedora. He stood tall and proud even though his face, hair, and hands showed the effects of old age. Confused for only a second, she then recognized him.

"Grandpa Otis?" She questioned with a furrowed brow. "Is that you?"

"Yes, Millie," He replied smiling, "It is."

"But... you're dead!"

Alfred Otis laughed as he replied. "Well... so are you, my dear child! And you've never looked better." He took her hand in his. "I'm here to welcome you home."

"Home?" she whispered. She then looked around. "Where is this place?"

Alfred smiled. "Don't you recognize it?" Alfred asked, his voice tinged with a warm German accent. "This is the apple field on my land in Atchison!" He then gestured with his arm. "The very trees you climbed with your sister Pidge when you were both very young." The scent of fresh earth and sweet apples warmed her soul. She smiled as memories flooded back. She watched as a bright pink butterfly fluttered by, its delicate wings dancing in the sunlight. With a gentle gesture, Amelia held out her hand, feeling the butterfly's delicate touch as it perched upon her palm. She remembered the dragonflies hovering in the field, their iridescent wings shimmering in the breeze. As she watched it fly away, she said. "I don't remember them being so beautiful!"

"Everything here is beautiful!" Alfred replied. In the blink of an eye, she stood in her grandfather's simple living room. The familiar sights brought comfort. Sitting in the corner, the worn banjo she learned to play as a child caught her eye, its strings gleaming in the soft light. As she picked it up, the coolness of the steel strings against her fingertips brought back a flood of memories. With only a moment's thought, she effortlessly played the first song she had ever learned, the notes filling the room with a melody of nostalgia. Her grandfather's joyful applause echoed in her ears, bringing tears of joy. He approached her, his arm wrapping around her in a comforting embrace.

He gently kissed her forehead and whispered, "You're home."

Confusion crossed Amelia's face as she furrowed her brow. "Is this Heaven?" she asked.

Alfred chuckled softly. "No, my dear, It's the waiting place."

"Paradise?"

"Yes, some call it that." He said with a smile.

She turned from him and then questioned, "Is there more?"

"What more would you like?" Another familiar voice rang out. As Amelia spun, she saw a tall, slender woman standing on a runway in a long black leather jacket, pants, and a white silk scarf. Behind her was a Curtiss JN-4 Canuck biplane.

"Nita?" Amelia cried out in surprise. "Nita Snook?"

She replied. "Yes, Amelia, It's me!"

Amelia laughed, "I haven't seen you since you taught me to fly in 1921."

"Have you enjoyed flying?" Nita inquired.

Nodding, Amelia replied. "Oh yes, with all my heart!"

"That's good. I'm glad I could bring you such joy."

"Thanks to you, flying has brought me more happiness than anything else I've ever done!" Then, as quickly as it had appeared, the world before her faded into a stark white void. The warmth she had experienced in her plane as it entered the light now fell upon her again and brought peace and contentment to her soul. In the distance, a lone figure walked out of the whiteness. As he drew near, he said.

"Welcome home, my child," Jesus said, his voice filled with warmth and love. Amelia's eyes filled with tears as she recognized Him, the sight of his scarred hands bringing forth a flood of emotions. With a gentle nod, he extended his hands towards her, beckoning her forward. As she took hesitant steps towards him, sobs of overwhelming joy escaped her lips. She finally fell into his waiting arms, feeling the strength they provided. Jesus, his touch bringing a soothing sense of relief, gently wiped away Amelia's tears. His voice, soft and comforting, broke the silence.

"You didn't answer Nita's question," he whispered. Confusion furrowed Amelia's brow as she looked into his humbled eyes. Jesus lifted her chin with his fingers, guiding her gaze to his.

"What?" she questioned.

"You didn't answer Nita's question. What more would you like?" he repeated, his words filled with curiosity.

Wiping her eyes and stepping back, Amelia's voice trembled as she questioned, "I have a choice?"

Jesus chuckled, his laughter warm and soothing. "Of course you do," he affirmed. "The plan of happiness is all about free will and choice." As she stared into his eyes, a newfound determination filled her.

She asked, "What are my choices?"

Jesus took a moment before answering, his smile filled with understanding. "Well," he began, "stay or go, up or down, right or left, in or out... it's all up to you. It's your choice." His words resonated within her, stirring a sense of empowerment.

Amelia couldn't help but laugh, her joy bubbling forth. "I've always strived to push myself beyond limits, to be the best version of myself," she confessed. "Can't speak for others, but I don't want to simply exist here in my memories. I want to keep doing things, to feel useful and needed." Jesus nodded, acknowledging her desires.

"Agency is the name of the game, Amelia," he said. "Tell me, what would you like to do for time and all eternity?"

Contemplating for a moment, Amelia's eyes lit up with excitement.

"I can't imagine myself just sitting around playing a harp until the resurrection," she shared. "Is there anything else I can do to serve you?" She smiled as she continued, "Perhaps you need an experienced aviator to fly you around?"

Jesus chuckled, the sound filling the air. "No, not really," he replied. A brief pause ensued before he spoke again. "In the past, I have allowed some to return to the earth as translated beings to help others. I believe I have the perfect job for you. I could send you back to be a Guardians of the Exodus member!" Amelia's eyes widened with excitement.

"Wow," she exclaimed, unable to contain her joy. "That sounds exhilarating! What do I have to do?"

Jesus took her hand, intertwining their fingers, as they began walking together. "You'll ride around on a horse and live in a tent with a bunch of stinky goats," he said with a playful tone.

Amelia couldn't help but laugh. "Sounds like fun," she replied, her enthusiasm evident. "Sign me up!"

With her story now told, Amelia's memory faded away. As she returned to the present, she turned to Storm and smiled.

"When I first got back to earth, I was shown where the staff of Moses was on Mount Sinai and told to place it within the temple of Sin to keep it safe and hidden for all eternity. Unfortunately, thanks to you two, eternity only lasted seventy-five years." Looking to Walsh, Jehorum grimaced.

"A lot of good that did us!"

"Hey... that wasn't our fault!"

"Was, too!" Jehorum stated.

Amelia then turned to face them and folded her arms. "Do I have to come over there and separate you two?"

Brenda laughed, "Yeah, well... sorry about that."

Amelia then said. "No harm done. It's even more hidden now, anyway."

Walsh turned to face her. "So, will He ever give the treasures of the Exodus back to man?"

Amelia shook her head. "I don't know that. But the Lord has said that everything has its seasons under heaven."

Brenda looked up as the first stars of the night twinkled in the twilight. "So, what happens next?"

Amelia's shoulders rose and fell. "Go on doing what the Guardians have been doing for four thousand years." She looked at Jehorum. "I'll be here until the second coming, if not longer."

Yadin shook his head. "Sounds like a lonely life to me."

Slapping Jehorum on the back, Amelia laughed, "Not at all. All the Guardians of the Exodus have dedicated themselves and their family's past, present, and future to the Lord's work. I'm in great company!"

As Jehorum climbed back on his horse, he pronounced, "We must go now. And so must you!"

Brenda stood and embraced Amelia. "Will we ever see you again?"

Amelia smiled as she pulled away. With a wink, she replied, "Only if you get too close to something you're not supposed to see!"

Brenda laughed, "Well, in my line of work, that might happen sooner than you think!" As Amelia remounted her horse, Brenda waved goodbye. "I'm glad this all had a happy ending for you!" Amelia then waved back and smiled.

"I'm happy, really, really happy." She added, "And man, is that he should have joy."

• • • •

EPILOG

Early the following morning, Brenda awoke to the melodic sound of the Beatles' song 'Here Comes the Sun.' As she slowly opened her eyes, the warm embrace of the day greeted her through the tent flap. With a deep frown etching across her face, she instinctively pulled the soft pillow over her face, muffling her scream of frustration. Walsh cried out in disbelief somewhere outside, his voice filled with a sense of urgency.

"It's gone! The plane is gone!"

Brenda's heart raced as she ripped the pillow from her face and shouted in response, "What?" Jumping up from her sleeping bag, she dashed out of the tent, her bare feet sinking into the cool, soft sand beneath her. The vibrant orange glow of the canyon engulfed her as she joined the others, their eyes fixed on the spot where the plane had once stood.

Yadin's voice trembled with confusion as he questioned, "Where did it go?" Brenda cautiously approached the area, scanning the sand for any traces of the plane's landing gear, but found nothing.

Brimmer's voice cracked as he joined her, "There's no sign of it ever being here!" He then smiled. "Maybe it was never here in the first place."

Storm turned abruptly, her anger rising. "What are you talking about?"

Brimmer's voice held a hint of uncertainty as he replied, "Just that... maybe we all just imagined the whole thing."

Walsh, now standing with them, scoffed at the idea. "Mass delusion? That's just crazy!"

"Is it?" Brimmer asked. "Is it any less crazy than us believing that we've talked to someone who has been missing and hasn't aged in seventy-five years?" Brenda's brow furrowed as she pondered his words. Brimmer's voice grew quieter as he added, "Or the fact that time can stop inside an airplane?" He shook his head, a sense of unease in his eyes. "The whole thing sounds crazy to me."

"Maybe that's what Amelia meant," Yadin said as he walked to join the group.

"What do you mean?" Brenda questioned as she faced him.

He then said, "She said it wouldn't matter if she told us everything because no one would believe us, anyway."

"But we still have proof, even without the plane," Walsh said with a smile. "All the pictures I took, uploaded information, the dragonfly…"

Suddenly, everyone stared at each other momentarily and then cried out simultaneously. "Noonan's body!" Storm and her group began running toward the operations tent with great urgency. Tearing through the flap, they pushed through the plastic curtain and stood looking down at the now-empty examination table.

"It's gone!" Yadin exclaimed, his voice filled with sadness, the weight of disappointment evident in his slumped shoulders. He knelt and peered under the table, his eyes scanning the space. "The body is... gone."

Brimmer's lips curled into a sly smile as he said, "What body?"

Brenda's fury surged, causing her to whirl around in anger. Her voice erupted in a yell, filled with frustration, "Will you please stop that?" She shook her head in disbelief, her hair swaying with the force of her motion. "It was here!"

Walsh then chimed in with a smile, "Was it?"

Brenda furrowed her brow. "Oh, no! Not you, too?"

Walsh let out a hearty laugh, his amusement evident. "How much you wanna bet that every shred of information we've collected over the last four days was erased from existence!" He leaned in, his expression knowing. "I work for the CIA; I know how this kind of thing works." Brenda's frustration escalated as she stormed towards the main laptop. The sound reverberated through the tent, filled with a sense of desperation. She frantically searched through the files, her fingers tapping quickly on the keyboard. But as she scrolled through, the screen displayed nothing but emptiness. A scream escaped her lips as a cry of disbelief and unacceptance. Determined, she then moved on to her internet storage site as her heart pounded in her chest. She accessed her account with a feeling of anticipation. But it shattered her hopes as she discovered that it, too, was devoid of any evidence. Even the emails she had sent, the digital trail of their findings, had vanished. It was as if all their meticulous research had never happened. Brenda slumped back in her chair, her eyes meeting Walsh's with a combination of defeat and desperation.

"It's all gone. Every shred of evidence."

Brimmer sat beside her, his presence offering a small glimmer of support. He spoke, his voice tinged with concern, "If we try to tell people what happened here without proof..."

Brenda finished his sentence, her words cutting through the silence in a frigid tone, "They'll give us all a one-way ticket to the funny farm." A heavy silence settled in the tent, the weight of their predicament pressing down on them.

Yadin turned to Brenda, his voice filled with uncertainty. "So... what are we going to do now?"

After a moment, Storm's face lit up with a mischievous grin, her eyes twinkling with excitement. "I just happen to know where the lost city of Atlantis is..." She spun on her heel and started striding towards the camels. "Last one there is a rotten egg!"

••••

The End?

ABOUT THE AUTHOR

After surviving a major heart attack in 2022, Michael E. Coones decided to reevaluate his life and what he had done with it. He was not pleased with what he found. Somewhere along the line, he had lost touch with what was truly important to him: his family, and his relationship with God. While the Lord blessed him with God-given talents, he had not utilized them to spread the gospel and bring souls to Christ. He has since dedicated his life to this mission.

Michael E. Coones lives in Orem Utah with his eternal companion and wife, Nancy. He is the father of 5 children.

Other Books by
Michael E. Coones

Available on Amazon

Brenda Storm - Finding Excalibur

Commander Courage
and the Lost Planet Airmen

Commander Courage
and the Forgotten Books of Darkness

The Liberty 9 Miracle

Made in the USA
Middletown, DE
27 June 2024

56401304R00106